His finger brushed over her cheek and then pushed a strand of hair behind her ear.

"I'm sorry I cornered you. You're too good at revealing nothing of yourself, and I want to know more."

"For the mission," she said, still not opening her eyes because she was afraid if she did he'd stop touching her.

"No," he said.

His forehead rested against hers, and the softness of his exhalation brushed over her mouth, making her lips tingle. She did open her eyes then. He was so close. Their eyes met and she realized she was holding her breath, waiting for something. Waiting for him to make the next move.

Waiting because she wasn't sure of herself with him. Which was so unlike her that she put her hand on his jaw. He'd shaved, so the skin was so smooth she couldn't help running her finger over it. Then she tipped her head to the side, reached up and kissed him.

A real first kiss. Not one for show but one that they both wanted. One that was just for the two of them.

Dear Reader,

Price Security has grown so much from my initial idea of writing a billionaire's bodyguard. Honestly, it's been so much fun to explore all of the people who work for Price Security. Lee Oscar's not a bodyguard per se, but more of a security operative who is most comfortable sitting behind her bank of computers watching over everyone and gathering intel.

So I knew she needed to be pushed out of her safe zone and into the real world. What starts out as a favor to a friend drags her into the undercover operation of Aaron Quentin, Xander's hot brother, who Lee has been ignoring since they first crossed paths in Miami. But there is no ignoring him when he spots her at a club he's just been placed in, and to protect them both, they fake being a couple.

Being undercover and trying to find a missing girl is enough stress for anyone, but fighting her attraction to Aaron makes it even more challenging for Lee.

Aaron is happiest when he's undercover and pretending to be someone else. He's responsible for an accident that left one of his brothers paralyzed. So he's careful...very careful. Until suddenly he's Lee's pretend man, and he knows deep down he wants that to be real.

I loved writing this story. These two characters were so much fun to explore. Thanks for picking up this book!

Happy reading,

Katherine

FIND HER

KATHERINE GARBERA

ROMANTIC SUSPENSE

**Harlequin®
ROMANTIC
SUSPENSE™**

Recycling programs for this product may not exist in your area.

ISBN-13: 978-1-335-50267-4

Find Her

 Harlequin Enterprises ULC
22 Adelaide St. West, 41st Floor
Toronto, Ontario M5H 4E3, Canada
www.Harlequin.com

Printed in Lithuania

MIX
Paper | Supporting responsible forestry
FSC® C021394

Katherine Garbera is a *USA TODAY* bestselling author of more than one hundred novels, which have been translated into over two dozen languages and sold millions of copies worldwide. She is the mother of two incredibly creative and snarky grown children. Katherine enjoys drinking champagne, reading, walking and traveling with her husband. She lives in Kent, UK, where she is working on her next novel. Visit her on the web at www.katherinegarbera.com.

Books by Katherine Garbera

Harlequin Romantic Suspense

Price Security

Bodyguard Most Wanted
Safe in Her Bodyguard's Arms
Christmas Bodyguard
Find Her

Visit the Author Profile page
at Harlequin.com for more titles.

To Ryan and Rachel, who are just starting their life together. I hope it's full of love, laughter and happiness.

Love, Aunt Kathy

Acknowledgments

I'm so lucky to be a writer and get to spend every day at my desk living in story worlds that I create. Thank you, reader, for allowing me that.

Also thank you to Joss Wood and Tina Maria Clark. I do writing sprints with them every day, which keeps me on track and gives me a place to just chat on my breaks about the world and writing.

Chapter 1

Lee Oscar didn't do regrets. She might have had a different life if her best friend, Hannah Johnson, hadn't gone missing two weeks before they graduated from high school. If she spent too much time dwelling on those mistakes, then she went down a rabbit hole that led to pain and destructive tendencies.

However, Boyd Chiseck was one of those people who *did* regrets. Hannah's disappearance when they'd all been seventeen had forged that in both of them. After living through that, Lee had learned there was no one who could keep her safe except herself. And had decided from that point on to arm herself with skills, both lethal and technical, to fight evil in this modern age.

She spotted him right away. He was just under six foot and had broad shoulders, but the years had softened his shape, giving him a bit of a dad bod even though he'd never had children. Boyd kept his brown locks trimmed short, but he still had a full head of hair even though he was in his forties. Her attention shifting to his face, she took in his neatly trimmed beard and preppy clothing. Today he was adorned in neat dark jeans that he'd probably pressed and a Ralph Lauren polo shirt.

His eyes were brown, not really remarkable except that he always had an intensity and sadness about him. The two were inexplicably twined, and whenever Lee sat across from him, she almost felt the weight of those emotions.

For Boyd, he'd gone into protection mode. Trained as a teacher while Lee had been going through training for an elite intelligence agency based in the US. Both of them determined to help people when they hadn't been able to save their good friend Hannah.

So when he called out of the blue asking her to meet him for coffee… Well, her first emotion wasn't excitement or nostalgia for catching up with an old acquaintance. Because Boyd would forever be tied to that one moment that had shaped her into the woman she was today.

At forty-two, she might have fooled herself into believing that what had transpired twenty-five years earlier would always stay firmly in her rearview, but as she walked into Zara's Brew, she knew that wasn't the case. There was never going to be a time when she and Boyd met up that Lee didn't remember Hannah Johnson and wish she'd done things differently.

But a seventeen-year-old's worldview was a lot different than a grown woman's.

He waved when he saw her and she moved through the café to take a seat at the booth that he'd selected. He had no way of knowing that she'd watched a shoot-out take place in that very booth six months earlier when her coworker and friend Kenji Wada and his fiancée, Daphne Amana, had been ambushed while the international rights lawyer had been trying to get evidence in a case she'd been working on.

No regrets, the voice in her head said dryly.

But, in reality, there always were. She'd been monitoring all the cameras and wasn't sure how she'd missed the sniper that had set up on the far side of the parking lot.

"Hiya. I ordered you an Americano with three sugars," Boyd said after he'd stood to give her a hug. "Told them to bring it when you got here."

"Thanks. Been here awhile?"

"Not really. You know me…thirty minutes early always feels late," he replied.

That hadn't always been the case, but she understood why it had become his habit. "I do. So you mentioned you needed some help."

"No small talk?" he murmured dryly. His dark brown hair had grayed over the years, and he was still in shape but not as muscled as he'd been when he played on their high school football team.

"How's the family?" she asked, a tinge of heat rising to her cheeks. "Sorry. I pretty much spend all of my time at my desk with monitors around me and only talk to the team when giving recon info or issuing a warning or order."

"Fair enough," Boyd said. "Parents are good. Dad finally retired and Mom is trying to push for that move to Arizona. We'll see what happens."

"And Daniella?"

"Good… I hear she's good," he muttered.

Lee lifted both eyebrows.

"She left about six months ago. I see her at work but

we're separated," he told her with a shrug. "Mom suggested maybe marriage isn't for me."

"Wow. Sorry about that," Lee said. Daniella had been his third wife.

"Me too. She said I can't let go of the past."

Lee nodded. This wasn't news. She and Boyd both knew that he couldn't. That he would always blame himself for staying late at the gym to hang with the guys instead of going to meet Hannah. He'd always wonder if had he been there for his girlfriend she might not have been taken and would still be alive today. Lee wondered the same thing but about herself. If she'd left the computer lab with Hannah and gone to wait for Boyd with her instead of trying to get the program language for the algorithm she'd been working on to track grades and prove that her English teacher graded down on girls...

She reached over and squeezed his hand. There wasn't really anything she could say that would make him feel better. Or herself, for that matter. "So..."

The barista dropped off Lee's drink and then Boyd leaned closer. "One of my students hasn't shown up to class for the last three days. She has a rough home life and I'm not sure what happened. She might have run away. I called the number on file for her mom but haven't received an answer."

Lee wasn't exactly surprised by this. Boyd had come to her before when he thought things were odd with a student. "Name."

"Isabell Montez, but she goes by Izzie."

She pulled out her smartphone and started making notes on the notepad. Boyd gave her a physical description and AirDropped Izzie's yearbook photo to her. "I went to the cops and they said they'd do a wellness visit to her home," he added. "But I haven't heard back from them."

"Did you go by the house?"

He nodded. "I did. There's no sign of anyone there. I think the cops will probably just write it off, but my gut says there's more here."

Because of what they'd both been through, his gut was always going to say that, Lee realized. "Okay. I'll check into it. Does she have socials?"

He shrugged. "No clue. That's not really my thing."

Why did that not surprise her? Boyd wasn't exactly the Facebook type. "Fair enough. I'll check into this and get back to you when I hear something," Lee said.

He flashed a quick grin. "Which *is* your thing."

"What do you mean?"

"Just that you only come out from behind your computer when there's a crime to solve and then you go back."

She shrugged, not really able to argue with that.

They'd already exhausted the small talk, so she took a quick sip of her sweet, dark brew and then nodded at her old friend and got up, ready to start digging into Izzie Montez to find out where she'd gone.

A new puzzle to solve and hopefully a girl that could be saved. Van would say she'd joined Price Security to rescue people. Hell, everyone on the team had done that. But this time because Boyd was involved, the need to get this right and find that girl was stronger than it had been in a while.

Aaron Quentin liked life undercover. He didn't need a therapist to tell him that he used his work to hide from life. He knew that. However, over the last year, he'd started to get closer to his youngest brother, Xander, which was making him reevaluate some things.

He was British but worked for the DEA on their large criminal-gangs task force. Aaron had originally come to work for the DEA when he'd been on holiday in Miami. He'd been at loose ends, making money fighting in some underground clubs, when a fellow fighter had introduced him to his backers who were part of an East Coast drug syndicate.

Aaron had realized he was at another crossroad, and for the first time in his twenty-eight years, he'd decided to do the smart thing and not screw up again. He'd used a contact he had from his time in the SAS to get a meeting with a local DEA agent, and that had been it. Now ten years later, he was almost feeling like the work he'd done taking down two large criminal networks almost made up for the angry, tough youth he'd once been.

The accident was something he'd never be able to forgive himself for, and his family would never fully be healed. But looking at forty gave him a different perspective. Seeing Xander settled with his fiancée, Obie Keller, and working in private security was also helping. Also, having his brother back in his life… Well, it was making Aaron see his life through a different lens.

There was always that question of how long he could be effective undercover. He'd come out to the West Coast because after a high-profile bust in Miami, he felt he was getting too well-known.

Or at least that's what he *told* himself. The other reason, which he wasn't ready to delve into, was to be closer to Xander. The two of them, along with his future sister-in-law, had all gone home for Christmas. It had been… eye-opening to realize how much he'd missed the family, and after a long chat with Tony, he was starting to see himself in a different light.

Of course, it wasn't as easy as it always seemed on TV shows or in movies. The truth was, violence was where he was most comfortable—or had been. That's why undercover work suited him. He had no issues being a tough guy, or fitting in with the criminal element.

They were his people. He understood what it was like to grow up in a crowd of testosterone and always fight to be the alpha. He was the third of four brothers who'd grown up wild.

He and Xander were the youngest and their older brothers never pulled punches. He'd learned to be resilient and to survive by example. Fighting to be the top dog was all he'd known until a rugby game where his second-oldest brother was left paralyzed after a tackle by Aaron.

He'd blamed himself. Hell, they all had in different ways. Could Tony and Abe, the older two, have stopped antagonizing him and Xander? Couldn't he and Xander have just walked away? Sure, but that wasn't the Quentin MO.

Aaron blew out a breath. All this wading through the past was making his skin feel too tight and itchy, had him wishing he could just down a bottle of whiskey to forget. But he hated being drunk and how that thin veneer that he called control would often slip away and he'd wind up in a fight—because he *always* did—and then would most likely add to his list of regrets.

As much as he'd told himself he was in LA because of Xander, he knew there was another reason. Lee Oscar.

She was the tech genius at Price Security. Hot as hell…as much as he didn't do romance because of his job and basic lack of good relationship skills. Still, he couldn't shake her from his thoughts.

She wasn't his usual type of woman, which didn't mean crap to his libido. Apparently faded tight jeans and T-shirts that skimmed her curves were what he was attracted to.

"Mate, what are you doing here?"

Aaron glanced over his left shoulder to see Xander striding toward him. His brother was just coming off a job—Price had let Aaron know and also let him into the building. He'd been waiting in what served as a guest lobby on the fourth floor.

"Hoping for some hang time. Obie called."

Xander rubbed the back of his neck as he dropped his duffel on the floor at his feet. Aaron walked over and hugged his brother. Not for a moment embarrassed by the emotion that swamped him. He'd been alone for too long.

"Yeah? I can hang. Gotta shower though, and Kenji and I have a *Halo* match."

Price Security was so much more than a workplace. Giovanni "Van" Price had created a family out of the loners he'd hired as first-rate bodyguards and security consultants, something that Aaron had seen firsthand in Miami.

For a moment, he was jealous of the found family that Xander had here. But then shoved that down. He was slowly trying to rebuild the brotherly bond that he'd ripped the hell out of when they'd been in their early twenties. "Cool."

"Great. Let's go up to my place. You in town for work?"

"Yeah. I start on Monday. Trying to lie low. Was going to hole up in a hotel but then...Obie."

"You didn't have to wait for her to call. You can always crash at my place," Xander said.

Aaron shrugged. He still wasn't used to this either. He'd made himself into a lone wolf after his pack had disintegrated. Convinced himself that he liked it better that way. But recently he was beginning to rethink it.

Starting to want to see Xander and his family more often. And wondering if maybe there was a different life out there for him.

When they got on the elevator, Lee Oscar was on there. Their eyes met and she lifted one eyebrow when his gaze lingered too long. Lee was about five-five and fit. She had long brown hair that she habitually wore pulled back in a ponytail and was whip-smart.

He'd talked to her in Miami after she and the rest of the Price Security team had helped him wrap a delicate case he'd been working. He'd noticed her as a woman the very first moment he met her. He leaned against the wall of the elevator, crossing his legs at the ankle as he watched her, trying to figure out what was different about her.

"Hey, babe, how's life treating you?" he asked. Noticing his brother shaking his head. But Xander hadn't been there in Miami when they'd done shots of tequila, and for a moment in the hot moonlight, something had passed between the two of them.

"Fine. You, babe?" she asked.

He noted Xander trying to hide a smile but ignored his brother.

"Same. Just starting a new gig."

"Are you staying here?" she asked him, not Xander.

"Do you want me to?" he asked. If she ever gave him the hint of an opening, he'd jump at it. But with Lee, it was like he had no game. None. Other women usually took one look at him and it was game on. But not Lee.

"Not really," she said.

"Ouch."

"Sorry. It's just your job is high-risk and it would mean extra security measures in place and that's more work for me."

"I don't want to cause that," he said. "Plus I'm undercover, and this building is a bit too high vis for my MO."

"Another case like Miami?" she asked.

"Something," he said. He couldn't divulge the details and didn't want to. His life worked because of the compartments he kept.

"Be safe," she said as she exited on her floor.

"You too, babe."

She paused, glancing back over her shoulder. "It's Lee, not babe."

He gave her a slow smile and arched one eyebrow at her. "Noted, Lee."

"Mate, seriously?"

"Seriously."

"She's not a casual-type woman," Xander said. "She's like a sister to me, so watch yourself."

"She's got her own back," Aaron said. He wondered if he should apologize to his brother but wouldn't have an idea where to begin. It was probably better he wasn't staying here.

Lee had his attention and it was clear that Xander wasn't down with that. But still he couldn't stop thinking about her... Something seemed different.

She looked worried. He hadn't seen her that way before.

Isabell Montez wasn't that hard to find. She had the regular socials and had been pretty active until about ten days ago. Thanks to Isabell's feed, Lee was able to pull together different photos and start running them through a facial recognition program that she had helped develop back when she'd been working for the government. She attended San Pedro High School, which of course Lee had been aware of since that was where Boyd worked. The program had been improved in the last fifteen years, and Lee had kept up with updates for herself and the government.

She thought about Boyd as she ran the search. That boy had never been the same after high school. She got it—she hadn't either—but it seemed to Lee that Boyd had been trapped in those four years. The good *and* the bad.

She couldn't get far enough away from her past. It was ironic that when she retired and started working with Van that she'd ended up only an hour away on the 5 from where she'd started her journey. Her grandpa had died a few years ago and Lee never went back to Ojai. She didn't want to. The past for her tended to stay there.

She was too busy doing her job and keeping her cli-

ents and the staff at Price Security safe. In a way, she
was the opposite of Boyd. Having had that one lapse
in judgment, she'd focused on never letting it happen
again. Her old classmate, on the other hand, felt as if he
were trying to fix what happened to Hannah. That if by
being vigilant he could bring her back. But that wasn't
ever going to happen.

Even though they'd never found her body, which of
course made things more complicated. Like, maybe she
was still alive. Though the years Lee had spent working
in human trafficking made her doubt that. She'd looked
for Hannah over the years. Had even used some software
to age her old pictures and run them through every facial
recognition program and came up with a few likenesses.

But they'd never panned out.

She stood and stretched as the program kept running,
when the door behind her opened. Her office was a bank
of computer screens and then, behind her, a big conference table that the team used when it was time to have
a confab or for Van to hand out assignments.

She glanced over her shoulder to see her boss walking toward her. Van Price was a big-muscled bald man
with intense green eyes that warmed when he laughed.
He wasn't tall, just presented himself in a way that made
everyone take a step back. When Lee had first met the
security guru almost twenty years ago, she'd been in-
timidated until they'd been paired on an undercover assignment and she realized that the tough exterior hid a
softy with a heart of gold.

She was one of a handful of people who knew that
fact, which she also knew was intentional. Van was lethal,

never hesitating to do what was necessary to keep his clients and his staff—or *family* as he called them—safe.

"How was old home week?"

She shook her head. "Painful. Boyd has another missing kid."

"*Another* one?"

"Yeah, every five years or so, he calls me about a kid he thinks has been taken," Lee said. Her mind naturally identified patterns, and even if they might be coincidences, she hadn't been able to ignore the fact that it was every five years since Hannah's disappearance that Boyd reached out.

"Was the kid taken?" Van asked.

"Not sure yet. I mean, the police definitely checked out her house after he called, and found nothing. The family was gone, so it could be they are just in the wind. But her socials went quiet too, which isn't normal for that age," Lee admitted. "So…what brings you by?"

"Just checking on one of my favorite girls," Van said, with that slow smile of his.

"Just checking in, huh?" She narrowed her eyes at him. "What do you need?" she asked, knowing Van never did anything without a reason.

"Kaitlyn Leo from the CIA reached out again asking for Kenji and Daphne's help. I thought we had an agreement. Can you look around and make sure they aren't active again?"

By "look around," he meant hack into the CIA's servers and check on the agent status. "Kenji would tell you."

"I know he would, but there is always a chance that Leo would go behind his back," Van grumbled. "We've both known that to happen."

They had. After they'd retired from the government, Kenji and Daphne had been asked to do favors, which both of them had agreed to, but then their status had been changed to active until they notified their bosses that they were definitely inactive.

"I'll let you know what I find. Aaron's here, by the way. I bumped into him in the elevator." She was still buzzing slightly from the interaction with him. He got her that way. That insolent way he leaned casually against the wall of the elevator and then checked her out in a manner that was anything but casual. Mixed Signals should have been his name.

There was a quiet intelligence to him that drew her, but then he opened his mouth and came on like someone who spent too much time in a bar. Which should have made it easier for her to ignore him completely.

But it didn't.

"Yeah, I gave him access. He's working in LA and needs a safe place for his downtime."

"Cool. A heads-up would have been nice," Lee said. Since she kept the building secure, she liked to know when they had someone new on the premises. Especially someone like Aaron Quentin who was usually deep undercover with drug cartels.

"He just arrived a little while ago," Van pointed out. "You sure you're okay?"

She knew she was touchy. It was Boyd and of course Hannah and this young girl, who'd looked funny and happy in her social media photos, who was now missing. Her mind could easily supply all the scenarios where she might be and how they could find her. It made her edgy.

She just shrugged.

Van put his hand on her shoulder and squeezed.

They both knew that there was nothing to be said. That world—the murky crime-filled one—continued to thrive no matter what they did and nothing would change that.

Lee's best hope was to find Izzie before too much more time passed.

Chapter 2

You only come out from behind your computer when there's a crime to solve...

Boyd's words sat in the back of her mind as she moved her fingers over the keyboard. It wasn't like her job had forced her to this position of observing everyone and everything. She'd had a rough upbringing and had learned early on to keep quiet and stay out of the way.

School had reinforced those behaviors, and four years in college and her recruitment by a secret government agency had finished the transition for her. She'd always been more comfortable observing and analyzing.

It was easier to make the tough calls when she wasn't in the field or interacting one-on-one with the person whose life was in her hands. But for some reason, tonight it didn't feel the way it usually had. Maybe it was the fact that Luna had gotten married and moved out of the tower.

Luna Urban-DeVere habitually wore her hair back in a tight ponytail. She had high cheekbones and a pert nose. Her eyes were worried when she met Lee's stare. Luna had been a solid hang, where they'd sort of sat in the same room and read together. Some people might not get that kind of friendship but for Lee…Luna was one of her besties, even if the other woman might not realize it.

Rubbing the back of her neck, she got up and walked to the kitchenette that was part of her setup at Price Security. She had a nice apartment across the hall but spent all of her time here in front of her computer monitors, accessing information and monitoring the team. Luckily she didn't need a lot of sleep—a solid six hours was all it took for her to feel refreshed, so she was ideally suited to be *overwatch* for Price Security.

The guys called her that sometimes. Well, Xander did because he'd been in the military. Rick dubbed her "chief" because he'd been a cop and then a DEA agent. He was used to a chain of command. Van was definitely the commissioner role.

Lee was sort of the glue that held everything together. She monitored everyone when they were in the field, relayed information as it came in, to different cases. No one asked her to do it 24-7, but it had sort of become her habit. At some point, she'd stopped dating and leaving the tower…like Boyd had mentioned, unless someone needed her.

She'd sort of lost herself in her work. It was safer when she was in the tower. Something she didn't allow herself to unpack.

She shook off whatever emotion was responsible for her melancholy as she made herself a cup of coffee and added a splash of skim milk. Grimacing as she did so. She liked coffee, even this version of her old favorite that she'd had to change as she got older.

She was resisting switching to decaf, even though the doctor wanted her to in order to cut back because of her acid reflux. She'd already given up sugar and cream to stop the spread of her hips, so it felt insulting that her body was now demanding she quit caffeine too.

Her computer pinged, which meant it had a hit, and she hurried back to her desk and sat.

She scanned the monitor she had running a search for Isabell's EID, embedded identity document. Basically it was a way to track the teenager's device without relying on the phone number. Since Isabell's phone wasn't responding to any calls and the girl had disappeared into thin air, Lee had thought to start this trace.

And she saw now it had pulled back a location that wasn't too far from here. Over in West Hollywood, in close proximity to Zara's Brew where Lee had met up with Boyd. She opened a map and tracked the location, switching to street view and noticing it was a club called Mistral's. It didn't look like a club for teens. So what had Isabell been doing there? How did an establishment that had hits on the internet from a teenager tagging the place not appear in any database?

Then she remembered that Van had asked her to make sure Price Security didn't show up on any map or internet tool for locations. Someone had also made sure that Mistral's wasn't on the map.

And the last ping of Isabell's phone was from there. She pulled up the file that Boyd had given her and searched for the cop's name who'd taken the report from him. It was someone she didn't know. She knew it wasn't Detective Miller's case, but she knew her pretty well from a couple of other cases.

Lee put in a call to Miller and then sat back in her chair. Looking again at the geotag on the social media posts, she used other sites around Mistral's to find the coordinates and then came up with a position.

One that she would check out tomorrow.

It was 4:00 a.m., just about time for her to head to bed. Lee left the other algorithms running and went across the hall to her apartment. Van had insisted she decorate it, so she'd bought some floor samples for a living and dining area and then a bed for the bedroom.

Lee had never really felt like any place was home. She had always carried it inside of herself. Plus, she also knew better than most that nice furniture didn't mean safety. So this sort of used stuff suited her.

She walked into her bedroom. Showering before hitting the hay was her habit, as was putting on her sleep headphones after climbing between the sheets. Bar sounds might not be anyone else's soothing sound, but it had always been for her. As a child, she knew she was safe sleeping in a backroom behind the bar with Grandpa working. Closing her eyes now, she could almost smell beer and cigarettes as she drifted off.

But what about Isabell, she wondered? Did that girl have any safety? From what Boyd had told her, the teen's home life wasn't great. But then that could be said of so many kids, and many, like her, had survived and didn't end up disappearing. So what had happened to this girl?

Tomorrow she'd start to unravel it. There wasn't a puzzle she couldn't solve given enough time. The team were all on relatively routine assignments, so Lee had time for this. She'd never shirk her duties, but Van always considered this type of job one that kept her skills fresh.

* * *

He'd had worse gigs, no denying that. Currently Aaron felt like he was inhabiting some sort of English version of what living in California was. He had a van that was on the beach and had been told to carry a surfboard. Except he couldn't surf and looked like a knob walking around with a board under his arm.

His boss wanted him to blend in, but he figured being a poser wasn't the right guy for this gang.

The Cachorros had been operating up and down the West Coast for more than a decade. Aaron had worked for the DEA for about the same amount of time. He'd primarily been based in Florida since that was where he'd shown up. But after he'd taken down a large crime network, his cover had been blown. His boss suggested it might be time for Aaron to get out of undercover work, but he wasn't ready for that yet.

So here he was, working his way up another crime cartel to get to the top. The street dealers were different in Cali than in Florida, but the same could be said of the differences between South London and Florida. Aaron was good at adapting and changing to meet the needs of any situation. He'd brought a lot of cash, made some big buys and started making waves when he'd first gotten into town a week ago.

He'd also found a mole from the Chacals, another crime organization, named Chico del Torro, and used him to move his way up. Chico was in charge of this seaside operation. Mainly overseeing sales on this stretch of the beach. There was a club at the end of the pier that was also owned by the gang and where Aaron had been hanging at night, trying to learn more about the organization.

To say that the Cachorros didn't really trust him was an understatement. And everyone was watching their backs around him. But that was fine with him. He was good at fighting and being a guy, so he knew how to bond over blood and beer. That was sort of his specialist skill. He could drink any of these Yanks under the table but he knew how to appear as if he'd had too much.

Like many of the people within large crime organizations, he didn't use the products they sold. Something that Aaron was grateful that he'd never been tempted into. Probably because he was one big rage machine underneath what he'd been told was a charming smile. He had known better than to add drugs to the mix.

"Boss wants to see you," Carmen said. "He's upstairs."

"Uh-oh. Am I in trouble?" he asked her, stealing some peanuts from the bar cups she was filling up.

She shrugged, tossing her long brown hair over her shoulder. "Do you *think* you are?"

"Sure hope not," he said with a wink before taking the stairs up to the office two at a time.

The boss was Jako Lourdes. He'd been the one who'd promoted him from street selling to running bags. The file that Aaron had read on him hadn't really matched the man he'd met. From the intel that the DEA had, he'd thought that Jako was just this big Pacific Islander who spent his time lazing around on the beach and surfing in between deals.

But in truth, he'd been implicated in a few hits on rival gang members. Though nothing had stuck. And the photos hadn't exactly been up-to-date. Something that Aaron had rectified. Jako owned several establishments in the small beach town of San Clemente. Most legit. Including one where the guy taught fire dancing and his sister taught hula.

So far, Aaron hadn't been able to figure out what the school was used for, but given that every other business Jako owned was doing something illegal, Aaron knew he was missing something.

He rapped on the door at the top of the stairs.

"Come in."

He entered the room and Jako was sitting on his desk, looking at his phone. Two of his closest were already there, both sprawled out on the leather couch. The room wasn't anything special. Faded wallpaper on the back wall that had been whitewashed and then had some basic graffiti of the gang's symbol.

"Quinn, my man. How's things?"

He always went by the name Quinn when he was working undercover. "Good. I think they're good. Completed the run and drop," he said.

"Yeah, heard that. You're efficient," Jako said.

"Try to be." Aaron was bigger than Jako and Roman, but not Steve, so if this went sideways, he figured he could take two of them but he wasn't getting out of here easily. Also mentally going over the last few days, he couldn't see where he'd have fucked up enough to warrant a beatdown.

"You are. I need you at another location. My bosses heard about the solid you did for me and they want to see what else you got."

Not what he was expecting. "Where am I going?"

"Los Angeles. That operation always needs new blood. The cops make our guys every few weeks and arrest them."

"I'm going back on the street?" Aaron asked.

"No. A club. Mistral's. We need you overseeing the operation. Someone got sloppy," Jako said.

Depending on how mucked up things were, Aaron wasn't sure whether he'd be able to clean this up. But he had worked in a nightclub in South Beach for four years, so at least a club was more his thing than surf shack on the sand. "I'll need to grab my stuff but can be ready to go in an hour." There wasn't anything keeping him in Cali except his brother…and Lee. Though it had been days since he'd seen her in the elevator, he was still replaying their interaction, wishing he'd been different but not sure how.

"Good," Jako said. "Make me proud."

"I will."

Aaron left the meeting knowing he couldn't risk checking in with his partner, Denis. He also suspected that this reassignment was more than what Jako had said. His bosses clearly wanted to be reassured about the kind of man they were getting in Aaron. This would be good for Jako, if he delivered. As for him? Well, it was getting him one step deeper into the organization, which was exactly what he needed.

Running algorithms on her computer was one avenue to explore, but Lee knew she also had to do some legwork. Which she was currently embroiled in. Sitting in the conference room, she had a map spread out on the table along with the records she'd managed to get from a contact that showed the different cell phone towers that had been pinged by Isabell's phone.

Stopping for a moment, she looked down at the girl.

She had long, curly hair that hung past her shoulders, her face was long and square, and her eyebrows on the thicker side, but Lee knew that was the trend nowadays. Her expression was solemn yet there was an air of maturity to her that belied her age. But…she was still a baby.

The picture that Lee was starting to put together of Isabell showed someone who was making choices that might have put her in danger. She had a meeting with Detective Miller later that day. She was going to introduce her to the man who was working Isabell Montez's case, Detective Monroe. It would be good to get some insight.

That said, cops were busy and this girl wasn't a top priority. And the fact that it was her teacher and not her parents who'd reported her missing was odd… Lee checked her watch. If she left now she could swing by the last known address.

The door to the conference room opened and Lee glanced up to see Luna coming in.

"Hey, girl."

"Hey. Van said you're working a side case. Thought I'd see if you needed to bounce ideas off someone," Luna said, coming over and putting a skinny decaf latte in front of her.

"Thanks. Actually, you fancy going on a field trip with me?"

"Sure. I'm between gigs for another week," she replied. "Where are we going?"

"I'll catch you up in the car," Lee said, grabbing her bag and her keys, keeping her coffee in the other hand.

"This the missing girl?" Luna asked, holding up the photo.

"Yes. Isabell Montez. She hasn't been to school in

ten days," Lee told her bestie as they took the elevator down to the garage and they headed to her black Dodge Charger. The entire team at Price Security drove them. They'd been special ordered with bulletproof glass and reinforced bodies. Not that she was anticipating trouble, but the car was fast and easily maneuverable. Something she appreciated in LA traffic.

"Ten days. That could be a lifetime," Luna said. "What did the cops say?"

Lee started the car after they got in and put on her sunglasses as she exited the parking garage onto Spring Street. She headed toward the Boyle Heights area where Isabell and her family had lived. "They looked into it, but the last known address looks like it's been abandoned, and when they questioned the neighbors, no one had seen them or heard anything." She huffed out a breath. "So they are playing wait and see."

"I hope they aren't waiting for a body," Luna muttered.

"I don't think so. They are overworked and the only one who's concerned about the girl is her teacher. They have feelers out with next of kin and are trying to track down her parents."

"Have you found them?" the other woman asked.

"Not yet. The cops put a bolo out for their car, but so far, nothing. I've also run the license and make through my visual recognition program, checking cameras at traffic lights and ATMs and anything, really, but again nothing," Lee said. "Which I don't like."

"I don't like it either. Cars usually get a hit. We heading to the kid's house?" Luna asked.

"Yeah. Just want to look around and see what's there.

The cops went and knocked on the door and looked in the windows and didn't see any signs of foul play, according to the report I read."

Luna arched a brow. "How'd you get the report?"

"I asked Detective Miller if she could help me out. And she did. It's public record so it's not like it's illegal," Lee said.

"Yeah, I know. I figured you just backdoored yourself into their files," Luna said with a laugh.

"Uh, no. Van doesn't want me doing that anymore. Kenji's boss from the CIA poking around last December made him wary of drawing any unwanted attention from the government. So…I'm trying. But, as you know, I am used to just getting what I want by any means…"

It wasn't that she couldn't appreciate that there were laws and they were meant to be followed. It was simply that when it came to criminal activity, the law was usually an afterthought. So she didn't like to hamper her own investigations by following rules that the bad guys were probably breaking.

"So. What are we looking for?" Luna asked when Lee pulled up in front of Isabell's house and turned off the car.

"I'm not sure. But *something*. That girl looks years too old to be sixteen. Something was happening here and…there are always signs," Lee said, remembering her own childhood.

Obviously she had no real idea if she was projecting her fractured parental relationship onto that picture of Isabell, or if the girl actually was in a hostile home situation. She just felt that by coming here and looking around she might get a better idea.

"Fair enough. Are we breaking in?" Luna asked.

"No, but if any of the doors or windows are open…" Lee trailed off.

Luna just nodded, and from the corner of her eye, Lee could see a slight smirk on her face as they both walked toward the house. Boyle Heights was an older neighborhood. Each of the yards had an overgrown lawn and the worn-out homes showed all of their years. And it was eerily quiet. No one was outside and there weren't a lot of cars on the street either. Lee shrugged. It was the middle of the workweek and workday. So that wasn't much of a red flag.

Luna moved to check the side yard and Lee was glad she had her friend with her. She'd missed working with Luna since her friend had quietly married billionaire Nicholas DeVere last February.

Lee moved up to the front of the house and paused. The front door had been kicked in and hung off its hinges. Definitely not the state it had been in when the cops had visited the first time.

She knew she had to call it in to the police.

"Uh, that doesn't look like no sign of foul play," Luna murmured.

"Yeah, exactly. You report it while I go poke around."

"Go on. But as soon as they say don't go inside, I'm going to mention my friend is in there and when they tell me to, I'll call you out," Luna said.

"That works for me."

She used her foot to open the door, pulling her weapon, not sure what might be waiting inside.

Chapter 3

Aaron and his partner, Denis, had been working for six months before they even hit the ground here in LA. It wasn't easy to find a way into a gang from the outside. Their boss wasn't even sure it was worth the effort and had warned them this might be a long-term gig.

Which suited Aaron. He liked disappearing into anyone who wasn't Aaron Quentin. He'd been working in San Clemente for a minor player before he'd finally had a chance to work his way into Jako's crew. The Cachorros squad was tight and didn't trust easily. Aaron had expected that and played it cool. Focusing on his position as a bagman for the organization.

Doing his runs, Aaron had noticed another member of the crew who was working for the rival Chacals gang. Which he'd used to earn Jako's trust and move up in the ranks. He wanted to be in charge of an operation so he could get access to the lieutenants. Aaron's investigation had led him and Denis to a shadowy figure who was known by one name. *Perses.* Jako hadn't mentioned him, but a member of one of the other gangs had one night when the dude had been drunk out of his mind.

Finally they had a lead. He'd been working low-level

organizations up and down the coast of California for months trying to find the one that would lead them to the person they were after. Their intel thus far led them to believe that drugs were just part of a bigger international operation. Aaron's boss at the DEA told him that there were other agents from an FBI task force also looking into Perses.

Steve had gotten Aaron to LA and then told him to meet him at a club called Mistral's later in the evening around seven. In the meantime, Aaron had gone back to his apartment—the one that the DEA had set him up in for his cover—and done some computer work. The rival gang member had worked for the Chacals and they ran their operation out of the Boyle Heights neighborhood of LA. He had trailed Chico to a drop house on Euclid before reporting back to Jako.

Jayne, his boss at the DEA, wanted him and his partner, Denis, to go and hit the place on Euclid and see if they could find any further evidence of that rival gang's operation.

Before heading out to meet up with his partner in West Hollywood, he checked the place one more time to ensure he had everything set up for tonight. This was his first step into the bigger world of the Cachorros gang. He wasn't going to screw it up.

He made sure he had his badge on a chain around his neck and tucked into his T-shirt and then walked out of his apartment. He kept his gun in the locked glove box of his van. He and Denis had comms, so as soon as he was in the vehicle, Aaron let him know he was on his way.

They were going to rendezvous at the house just in case Aaron had a tail. He'd have an excuse if Steve was following—he could say he was checking on the place where he'd last seen Chico make his drop.

He drove through traffic, focused on the job ahead, when he noticed a black Dodge Charger. Not really the kind of car that stuck out but he recognized it as one of the vehicles his brother drove for Price Security.

He drove past, checking to see if it was Xander, but saw a woman behind the wheel. Lee Oscar…he thought. He'd flirted with her hard the first time they'd met and she'd shut him down.

Fair enough.

Not everyone was into him, he knew, but he'd been intrigued by her. Hyperintelligent, quick-witted and never missing a beat. Not to mention the fact that Lee was an attractive woman. So was it any wonder that he'd been turned on by her? But at the same time, he wasn't just one big hormone. She'd said no and he respected that.

Didn't mean he'd been able to stop thinking about her. He was pretty sure she hadn't noticed him driving by, which was a good thing. He was on the job and really shouldn't be thinking about her curvy hips in those worn jeans she favored. Or the way she tipped her head to the side when he pushed too hard trying to charm her.

Everything about her just fascinated him, which was for another time. He signaled and got off the freeway, driving into an older, rundown neighborhood. The roads were quiet and he dumped the van in a park that had a swing set and merry-go-round. Two of the swings were fine but the third hung on one chain. He walked across the playground and noticed Denis waiting for him.

"Dude."

"The boss has SWAT standing by in case we uncover a

money-counting operation. They want to shut this down," his partner said.

"Got it," Aaron replied.

They moved in together, crossing the park before stopping at the second house on the block. It had a chain-link fence around the yard but the gate was open. There was music playing as they approached and two guys sat on the front porch in lawn chairs.

"Hey, uh, is Chico here?" Aaron asked.

That got their attention. They both sat up straighter and Aaron noticed one of the men pulling his gun up from his side.

"That's far enough," the other man said.

Lee entered the house and paused in the doorway. She heard Luna making the call, which meant that she had to be quick. The cops were right to tell her not to disturb the scene and she wasn't going to touch anything; she just wanted to see where Isabell had lived. Get an idea of the girl she was looking for. The living room smelled of old pizza and had been turned over, probably by whoever had broken in. Looking around, she noticed the cushions were off the couch and everything had been dumped.

Lee moved quickly down the hall past the kitchen. There was a bedroom on the right that was pretty nondescript and had been treated the same as the living room. Then another one, also containing a queen-size bed, with drawers dumped on the floor and an en suite bathroom. The last room on the left was smaller than the other two and had a single bed pushed under the window. The dresser drawers were open, but there were no clothes on the floor. In fact, it seemed like none of the furniture had anything in it.

This had to be Isabell's room. Had they already gotten rid of her stuff? Perhaps the parents had been hiding from the cops when they stopped by. It seemed odd to Lee that one room would be empty. Well, *this* room in particular, considering that Boyd was concerned about the girl.

Scanning the place further, she saw there was a poster on the wall of BTS, a K-pop band, and small desk that wouldn't have been out of place in Lee's own bedroom when she'd been a teenager. Someone had written on the surface in Sharpie.

Lee put on some medical gloves she'd brought with her before she ran her finger over the words. "This is just a phase." Then looked in the desk drawers, which were all opened. She tried to pull the top one out farther— it was stuck on its track—and when she did a Polaroid picture fell onto the base.

Isabell…but a very different, more mature-looking girl. She had on makeup and wore a choker around her neck. She was smiling at whoever was taking the photo, and it looked like maybe a bar in the background. Quickly, as she heard Luna calling her name, she took a photo of the Polaroid with her phone so she could reference it with the other pictures she'd found online.

"Coming."

She looked around, snapping photos of the writing on the desk and then took a quick peek into the closet. There was a jacket toward the back. A zippered army-green one that had a bunch of pockets with different patches sewn on it. She captured an image of it and then put her hand in the pocket, feeling around. She found a vape and some receipts, but they just had totals and not a retailer's name printed on them. She fanned them out on the desk and took a photo as Luna called for her again.

"Two minutes!"

"I'm almost done," Lee yelled back as she returned the stuff to the pockets and then turned, catching her foot on the bottom slider of the closet, which made her stumble. Before getting back on her feet, she glanced under the bed, remembering her own childhood home and the one place where she'd hidden stuff from her parents. Under the box spring of her bed. She lifted it up and found a file folder and, at the same moment, heard sirens. She wanted to look in that folder, but there was no time. She sprinted out of the house and slid next to Luna as the first cop car rounded the corner and pulled up behind the Dodge.

Luna turned and lifted one eyebrow at her. Lee knew she was asking if she'd found anything. She nodded.

The officers came up to the porch and asked them to step back to the sidewalk. Both women did. A second car arrived with two investigators. They came over to talk to her and Luna.

"Ladies. I'm Detective Monroe. What were you doing here?"

"I'm Lee Oscar and this is Luna Urban-DeVere. We're from Price Security and we've been hired to find a teenager who was living here," she said.

"Miller mentioned you were interested in the Montez girl. The place was like this when you got here?"

"Yes, sir," Luna said. "Clearly it's been vandalized. We called it in and waited as instructed."

"But if the girl's MIA, why did you come out *here*?" Monroe prodded.

"Wanted to see if the parents or the kid were back. It's been ten days since she stopped going to school. Something might have changed."

"Evidently it did," Monroe said, taking in the sorry state of the home.

"Yes. I'm not sure what this means. Maybe the entire family is in danger," Lee said. Though, based on what she'd seen, it was obvious that Isabell hadn't been living in this house for a while. Had she run away?

She blew out a frustrated breath. This fishing expedition had turned up more questions than answers.

"That's one of the things we will be investigating. I want you both to give a statement as to what you saw when you arrived. Can you come by the precinct later and do that?"

"Yes, of course," Lee said. Knowing from his tone that Monroe was dismissing them. "Any chance I can wait around and take a look inside?"

"No."

Well, okay then.

"We can talk when you stop by later. But this is an open investigation now, and I don't want anyone getting in the way," Monroe said sternly.

"Fair enough. We'll see you then," Luna murmured, taking Lee's arm and leading her back to the Charger.

Aaron launched himself the six feet toward the porch as he heard Denis doing the same. He knocked the gun from the guy's hand but was off balance. The momentum carried him forward and he rolled as he hit the ground, coming to his feet as the guy he'd rammed out of the chair followed suit.

He was a big, muscled man, and as soon as Aaron was on his feet, he took a punch to the throat, which hurt like a bitch. Retaliating, he struck his opponent hard with a front kick, catching him in the nose. Blood spurted on the other guy's face, hitting Aaron. But he ignored it as he followed the blow with a punch to the gut that sent the perp back against the front wall of the house, where his head hit on the brick before he slowly sank down to the ground.

Aaron was on him in an instant, rolling him to his stomach and wresting his hands behind his back to cuff him. He read the gunman his Miranda rights, glancing up to see Denis finishing up with the second guy.

"Front muscle down," Aaron barked into their comms, letting their reinforcements know that it was safe to approach. "Is the team in position?"

"We are. Go on your command," Harris responded.

Aaron glanced over at his partner, who nodded. They both drew their weapons before Aaron said, "Go!" and then kicked in the door. The house was dark with blacked-out windows and women in their underwear working money-counting machines. There were two guards at the front of the room and two at the back. Denis and Aaron each moved to take down the guards.

The fight was as quick and short as the one outside. Aaron used another kick combo that had the guards down and cuffed in seconds. The women who were working the machines didn't stop what they were doing until the power was cut and the machines turned off. Then they looked up before huddling closer together.

Aaron's boss took control of the scene, ensuring that the armed men and the women were escorted into vans for transport down to the police station. While that was all taking place, Aaron and Denis headed back to their vehicles. But as they got close, Aaron noticed a low-riding Dodge that he recognized but wasn't one of Price Security's.

"That's one of Jako's crew," Aaron muttered under his breath.

His colleague dropped back as Aaron tucked his badge under his shirt and kept his head down, walking a bit faster as if he was trying to distance himself from Denis.

Steve pulled up next to him. "What the hell are you doing over here?"

"This was where I tailed Chico, figured I'd make sure no one else was doing double duty. What are *you* doing here?" Aaron asked Steve.

"Same," the man said.

Which immediately made Aaron wonder if Steve had been running with both gangs. He decided to alert his boss and have him start tailing Steve to find out what was going on there.

"You get into it with them?"

"Yeah. Then the cops arrived and I beat it," Aaron said.

The gang member narrowed his eyes at him. "Cops? What kind?"

"I didn't stick around to find out. Are you going back to San Clemente?"

"Yeah. Figured I'd do a drive-by to where you said you saw Chico before I did," Steve said.

Again something about that was making the back of Aaron's neck itch. He nodded toward the other man before walking to his van as Steve pulled away. Denis had stopped at a bench in the park and looked like he was taking pills or something. But Aaron just got in his vehicle and started it up. They both had wireless comm devices that they wore in their ears.

"I'm heading toward the freeway, will double back and meet you at the station. Ask Jayne to tail that car. I'm not sure what he's doing in a rival gang's neighborhood."

"Will do. Let me know if you need an assist in losing him," Denis said.

"I won't."

"It's okay to ask for help," his partner reminded him.

"Yeah." He tapped his earpiece to mute it and continued driving toward the freeway, noticing that Steve was taking the same route. He signaled at Del Taco and pulled in. Steve just kept driving as Aaron got in the drive-through lane. His throat still ached from that punch he took. He ordered a Coke, which was sweeter in the US than in the UK, and then took his time leaving the parking lot. He headed back toward the freeway, looking for Steve's vehicle and saw it waiting in the McDonald's parking lot.

The guy was definitely up to something. But what?

Aaron drove past him, but when he pulled up at the traffic light, he saw Steve move into traffic behind him.

Great.

The light changed and he started to move again. He tapped his mic to unmute it. "I might have to go back to the apartment so my cover won't be blown."

"Go ahead. I'll see you soon."

Aaron got on the freeway, heading back toward his apartment in the Echo Lake area of Los Angeles. Steve took off as soon as they were on the freeway, and Aaron stayed in the slow lane, doing the speed limit. The gangster slowed down when Aaron got to his exit, no doubt making sure he got off where he'd said he was going. Once back at his place, he showered and changed before heading back to the police station to meet up with Denis.

It was late afternoon by the time he arrived, and he parked his van a few blocks away, walking the rest. He liked to have some distance between his cover role and his real-life one. It was easy to let the lines blur unless he kept them carefully drawn. When he got closer, he noticed another black Dodge Charger and glanced at the plates. Same one as earlier.

Lee was at the station.

Which really didn't concern him, but he stepped up his pace a little, hoping for a glimpse of the lady he couldn't seem to stop thinking about.

Chapter 4

Detective Monroe waved her over after she and Luna had given their statements. Luna had to leave to get back to Nick—they were hosting an event that night at Madness, the club her husband owned. Lee hugged her friend goodbye before heading to speak to Monroe. Given the workload she knew he had, she understood that the detective couldn't prioritize looking for Isabell over other cases that involved an obvious crime. After all, although the teenager was missing from school, there was no body and no one other than her teacher had reported her gone.

"Thanks for talking to me."

"No problem. Miller called over yesterday to ask me to speak to you about the Montez girl. We really don't have much to go on. The break-in at her last known address is something, but it doesn't mean a crime was committed. The parents work for WINgate, who has them listed for a month-long vacation. The B&E at their place might just have been opportunity."

She got that. "Or could the family have split because they owed someone money?"

"We don't know yet. I don't like how clean the girl's room was, but I don't know who else was living there. I have a deputy talking to the neighbors. But that neighborhood, no one notices anything, you know?" Monroe said.

She got it. She'd grown up in a suburb just like it. Everyone kept their heads down and minded their own business. "Did you find anything I could use to try to locate Isabell?"

He crossed his arms over his chest. "Not really. We dusted for prints at the house and I'm expediting reaching the next of kin to try to find out where the family is."

"That's good. So at least you'll know who was living there," Lee said. "And speaking of Isabell's relatives…" She pulled out her phone and opened a document. "I have her parents' names and have also compiled a list of Isabell's extended family. There's a maternal aunt in Cleveland and a cousin in Dallas. Want a copy?"

"Sure," he said, giving her his email address, and she forwarded the report to him. "Miller mentioned you were good with computers and tech. I'd say to focus your search there. If you find anything, bring it to me," Monroe said.

"Will do. And you'll do the same?"

He nodded tersely. "Oh, and one more thing…"

"Yeah?" she asked.

"I don't want to see you at another crime scene."

She took that as her signal to leave and got to her feet, heading down to give her fingerprints so they'd have them in case hers showed up at the crime scene. Which they shouldn't, since she'd been careful when she'd been in the house.

"Lee."

Turning, she came face-to-face with Aaron Quentin.

Despite herself, she couldn't help the way her pulse sped up. "Wh-what are you doing here?"

"Paperwork," he said. "Thought I saw you on the freeway earlier."

"Did you?"

He shook his head. "Lame. I have no game with you."

She laughed at the way he said that. "Because you try too hard."

"Is that it?" he asked, that British accent of his teasing her senses.

"Yes. Just chill out and stop trying to be a stud."

"I *am* a stud."

He was. No denying that Aaron was in top shape. Even though he was dressed in a T-shirt and jeans, the cotton fabric, while not tight, hugged his biceps. His jeans were the same, formfitting against thighs that were the shape of tree trunks. His eyes were blue and always seemed to be sparking with mischief. She let her gaze slide down his face to the square jaw that was clean-shaven and then she noticed a bruise forming at his throat.

"You okay?"

"Yeah. Rough day at the office."

"At least you didn't get arrested…or did you?" she asked, referencing when he'd called his brother for an assist after landing in jail in Miami.

"Not yet." He winked. "Actually, I was *making* an arrest."

"So you're not undercover right now?"

"I am. But I still have to do other parts of my job," he said. "It's not all working my way up the Cachorros."

"Maybe you can tell me about it sometime…"

"Yeah?" he asked, putting his arm on the wall behind her head and leaning in. "I'll tell you anything you want to know."

She smiled again. "Keep Mr. Hey Baby in check. I like you better that way."

"I'm just hearing you like me. So what are you doing here?"

"Tracking down a missing girl. Her last known address had a break-in, and Luna and I discovered it and called it in."

His eyes gleamed with interest. "Over in the Boyle Heights neighborhood?"

"Yeah, how'd you know?"

"Clocked you on the freeway heading that way and this police station is the nearest. You find the girl?"

"No, just a roughed-up house. No evidence of blood or a fight, and signs point to the girl leaving before the house had been tossed," Lee answered.

"That's a tough neighborhood. You think she ran away?" Aaron asked.

"No clue. Her teacher reported her missing, and her folks are gone, too, on an extended vacation…"

"Seems pretty straightforward. Like they cut bait and ran," Aaron said.

It did. She knew that the evidence was all pointing to that exact scenario, but that didn't sit right with Lee. Was she looking too hard for a crime that wasn't there? This was precisely why she usually stayed at Price Tower working the tech end of investigations.

But she couldn't rule out something dangerous happening to Isabell. Her gut, which had never let her down before, was telling her there was more here than she'd seen. She headed down to give her fingerprints.

* * *

When she got to her car, Aaron was leaning against the hood, waiting for her. She shook her head. *This man.* In Miami, when she'd first met him, they'd drank too much tequila and she'd contemplated making a bad decision. But in the end, the fact that he was the brother of a man she considered a brother... Well, she'd gone to bed alone.

But now he was in LA, hanging around and looking just like the distraction that she really needed.

"Can I help you?"

"Yeah. I need some tech help," he said.

Oh. She tried to tamp down her disappointment. Well, she *had* told him repeatedly that she wasn't interested in anything with him, so why should she feel let down now? But then again, he'd been flirting hard in the station and she had a little bit hoped... What? That he was going to ignore her earlier rebuffs? That was outdated early 2000s thinking and that twenty-year-old had matured.

Or so she'd thought.

"No problem. Want to follow me back to Price Tower?"

"Actually, I was hoping you could come to my apartment," he told her.

His apartment... It was for work, she reminded herself. But what did it say about her that immediately her body went hot and she was thinking about doing something reckless with him? Glancing down at her watch, she had an hour or so she could kill. "I can do that. What kind of problem is it?"

"I'll tell you when we're at my place. It's my cover apartment, so probably best if you look like someone I picked up when we get there," he said. "That work for you?"

"What do you have in mind?"

His piercing blue eyes locked on hers. "Just hand-holding, maybe a kiss…"

"Maybe?"

"You said no in Miami," he reminded her gruffly.

"I did. But maybe I've changed my mind," she demurred. Seeing that sad bedroom left behind by Isabell reminded her of where she'd come from and the glorious life she'd promised herself. Somehow during her twenties and thirties, work had taken over and she was still that same lonesome girl, just in a better living situation and with a better family, albeit a found one, around her.

"Which is it? Maybe? Or yes, you have?" he asked, straightening from leaning against the hood of her car to take one step toward her.

Though that one move didn't really lessen the gap between them, she knew it was his way of showing her he was interested too. Like she hadn't picked that up from all the times he'd tried his cheesy lines on her.

Biting her lip, she took a step toward *him*, wishing she'd picked up some sort of decent interpersonal skills over the course of her life that would help her seem seductive and, well, not like herself. "Yes."

He lifted both eyebrows and crossed his arms over his chest, smiling down at her. "Good. Very good."

Rolling her eyes, she wondered if this impulse was going to bite her in the butt, but she wasn't interested in changing her mind. It had been a long day…actually, a long year…maybe even decade. And she was tired of always staying safe.

But it wasn't physical danger she kept herself safe from, it was the internal injuries. Like caring too much for the wrong person, getting too involved in a case, those kinds of things that had made Lee start to feel like she was all alone in the world. And not really, truly engaged in anything.

Aaron closed the rest of the distance between them, and put his hand on her waist, leaning closer to her. "So kissing…?"

"Yes."

Before she could second-guess herself, he was lowering his head toward hers, blocking out the afternoon sun. The warmth of his breath brushed over her lips before the gentle touch of his mouth against hers. Her heart stuttered in her chest and she stood there, realizing how out of her depth she was with Aaron.

But then she shook herself. She wasn't. He was just a guy. A hot, *British* guy she wanted and had decided she was going to have. She shoved the scared teenager she'd been back into the box where she usually stayed.

Grabbing his shoulders, she shifted closer and then pushed her hand into the hair at the back of his head as she deepened the kiss. His mouth opened against hers, his tongue brushing against hers.

He tasted of coffee and mints…and something else. Something that she was pretty sure was just Aaron. His hands slid down her hips as he pulled her more fully against him. She felt his erection growing against her lower belly.

He lifted his head and their eyes met. She wasn't sure what he was looking for in her expression, but it was hard to hide the fact that she wanted him. That this lust had sprung between them and caught them both off guard.

It would be easy to say it was the frustration of the day or anything else, but the truth was she liked Aaron. She liked his big, hot, muscly body, his devilish smile, his eyes, which always looked like he was up to no good... And when that intense blue gaze was laser-focused on *her*, like it was right now...?

She was a goner.

Aaron reached out and stroked a hand through her hair. "I don't think this is going to be a hard charade to pull off."

"Me either. But I'm not playing a part," she whispered, because honesty was one thing she never compromised on.

"Yeah?" he asked.

She shook her head.

"I'm deep undercover, Lee," he said in a low, gravelly voice.

"I know. So we'll just keep it casual for now. I can't... I'm not good at keeping real life and a pretend scenario separate."

"Fair enough. Want me to get someone else to help with the tech? Xander's pretty good."

She didn't. She completely understood where Aaron was coming from and the fact that he'd told her straight-up instead of just going along with what she wanted meant a lot. "He'll just come and ask me."

Aaron laughed. "He's been helping me out when I need it, or was it you?"

"Me. He brings your stuff to me and I tell him how to do it."

"That dog."

"Yup. So I'll meet you at your apartment later?"

He nodded and with one final look her way, turned and went to his van.

Lee needed time to think. Some people would head to the beach, but for her it was always a walk around the Echo Park neighborhood in East-Central LA. There was a nice path around Silver Lake and one of her favorite taco trucks tended to park there. The neighborhood had become trendier in the last few years, but as far as she was concerned, it would always be the place that Grandpa had taken her for Swan Boat rides on Sunday mornings.

That girl she'd been... It was hard not to confuse Isabell with that youngster. Lee acknowledged she was seeing an abusive home for Isabell simply because that had been the reason Lee had wanted to run away. However, she'd never done it.

Hadn't had the courage. Lee had tried to improve the situation by going to the cops and filing a report. Calling them when her dad hit her hard enough to bruise her ribs and asking to be moved to a halfway house. Her grandpa had stepped in and taken her to live with him.

Lee had always relied on herself but she'd never wanted to be alone. She still didn't. Her family at Price Security were tight and everything she did was to keep them all safe.

It was the one thing she hadn't been able to do for her best friend, Hannah.

One of the few regrets she carried with herself.

Looking through the clues around Isabell's disappearance, it struck her that there weren't many at all. She got why the cops had put the case in the same category as other missing kids. There wasn't anything remarkable about it. Sad as that was to think and say, finding Isabell wasn't going to be easy.

It was even harder now that her parents weren't at their place. And had gone missing just like their daughter. Who were they? she wondered. Had they been like her parents and didn't give a shit about their daughter?

Or was it more complicated than that? Life was busy for everyone. It was part of the reason why Lee had never allowed herself to settle into a permanent relationship with anyone. It was hard to keep a bond strong with herself and anyone who didn't work for Price. That was where her focus always was.

Aaron was sort of an extension of her affection for Xander. Yeah, right. There was so much heat when she looked or thought about him that she'd made the decision to steer clear of him back in Miami.

Of course that was much easier when he was acting like he was *People*'s Sexiest Man Alive. Hell, he was too sexy for *People*. The last few years their selection had just been kind of meh.

Shaking her head, she got out of her car, tipping her head back to enjoy the Southern California sunshine. People were going about their regular lives, walking dogs, herding kids and going for runs. It should have made her feel lighter, but it didn't. There was no shaking Isabell Montez from her mind.

That teenager, who should be doing the same thing. Going to high school and hanging out with friends and hating one of her classes. Instead she was…where? Lee wished there was some way she could get in touch with that age group. But it had been years since she'd graduated and none of her friends had kids.

Boyd was the only one she knew with any connection to high school and she wasn't about to go back and talk to him again. Not right now. Seeing him just muddied everything as far as Lee was concerned.

She walked for about thirty minutes, clearing her head. The thing that had always served her was gathering information. That was what she needed to do. She'd start with the photo she'd taken from Isabell's desk; once she identified where it was taken then she'd have her next step.

Pulling out her phone, she looked down at the yearbook photo of the brown-haired girl with her face slightly rounded, probably still from baby fat, and those guileless eyes. What had happened to change her look into the girl in the instant photo?

That was what Lee had to unravel.

Her phone rang. Glancing at the screen, she saw it was Xander.

"What's up, X?"

"Aaron said you were helping him out. Thanks for that," Xander said in his slightly aristocratic British accent. He was a big guy who was normally pretty quiet. Wickedly smart and lethally strong, he was one of the best assets on their team.

"No problem. I'm giving him the family discount."

"Good. I owe you."

"You don't owe me. Aaron does," she retorted.

"Ha. You might be right."

Xander hung up as Lee got back in her car. Assisting

Aaron wasn't really a big deal. Kissing him… That was something else entirely. Friend-zoning him was a little bit for her own sanity since he was so hot and so aware of his charm. But also she didn't want to make things awkward between her and Xander.

The people at Price Security meant more to her than anything else. So if things got too heated or complicated with Aaron, well, that wasn't a risk she was willing to take. No matter how much she wanted to know what his mouth felt like on the rest of her body.

The traffic was intense, giving her more time to think before she headed toward Aaron's apartment to finish setting up the tech he needed her help with. The distraction from thinking about Isabell would be good. Lee always did better when she turned her attention in another direction and gave her subconscious time to work on the problem.

Chapter 5

Sitting at the dining table in his apartment, Aaron was determined to keep things professional with Lee. But the smell of her perfume, the air around them and each breath he took reminded him of how enticing this woman was.

She glanced over at him. "Is this making sense? Van constantly reminds me to keep it simple."

"Sort of," he said. Realizing he had to start paying attention to what she was saying instead of how her fingers looked moving on the keys. Her voice was sort of husky for a woman, but when she talked it was all business, which was totally turning him on.

He needed to get his body under control, because as he'd told her earlier, there was no place for this kind of relationship in his life at the moment. He had to continue doing his job investigating the Chacals as well as continuing his infiltration with the Cachorros. His partner and his boss were counting on him being the Aaron they knew. The guy who got his man and finished jobs.

"What's confusing?" she asked, turning to him.

You. You are confusing. "Why did you change your mind outside the police station? For months, whenever I run into you, you've been shutting me down."

She shrugged and he realized that she was hiding something too. Which wasn't a surprise. Everyone hid something. *Everyone.*

"I wish I could point to a reason and say it, but it was just sunny and you looked hot as usual and for once I just wanted to be the woman who said yes and took what she wanted."

He got that. He wanted her to take him. If they surrendered to their attraction, he'd give her everything he had. But it would have to end at being a hookup. Which wasn't wise for the two of them because she was tight with his brother, and unless Aaron wanted to walk away from Xander again, he was going to be bumping into Lee for the rest of his life.

"I'm undercover," he reminded her.

"I know. I did some undercover work when I was with the government. I get where you are coming from. It's hard to have a real life when the assignment has to be the priority." She sighed. "Just wish I didn't feel like this."

"Me too. But I've had a bit of time to think things over, and while I'm not saying no to exploring whatever this is between us, it's complicated."

"I get it. I don't want to be responsible for anything happening in your case," she said. "So…maybe we should just focus on business?" She pointed toward the screen. "What was confusing about what I showed you?"

"I'm not sure… I was distracted," he admitted gruffly. "Show me again please. I'll pay attention."

She looked like she was going to say something else but just bit her lower lip and then turned back to his laptop. He groaned to himself, trying not to focus on her mouth. "These are the cell towers that operate around the city, and the tracker that your partner put on Steve's car will ping it as he drives around. So right now, it is hitting one here."

Aaron stood up and leaned over her shoulder, putting his hand on the table next to the laptop. Looked like Steve was still in LA, despite the fact that he'd been heading south on the 5 the last time Aaron had seen him. "Can you get an exact location?"

"The nearest we can get is the tower and then we'd have to have a visual. But it seems like he's in this area. You could do a drive-by," she suggested.

"Good idea. Okay, so when he moves is there a way I can get a notification?" Aaron asked. Taking out his phone, he planned to text Denis and give him the area that Lee had identified. It was smack in the center of a neutral zone where neither of the gangs had sole territory.

Lee's fingers were moving on the keyboard and she glanced over at him. "Want the texts to go to you?"

"Can you send them to me and my partner?"

"Sure. Just give me the numbers. What do you want the notification to say?"

"Get fifty percent off pizzas if you order by 5:00 p.m.," he said. He and Denis used variations of food offers when they needed to get in touch with each other. "Will it send a location too?"

"It can, but given that you probably don't want to give too much away, I can make it so you log on to this site and get the update," she told him.

"Thanks, that works," Aaron said, walking over to the kitchen to call Denis and update his partner.

When he finished, he saw that Lee was gathering up

her stuff and getting ready to go. Which he knew was for the best. She'd helped him, she turned him on and they'd both decided now wasn't the right time.

For the first time ever, he regretted his job. He regretted that he'd made the choice to be a loner. He regretted that he was going to miss out on knowing her better. Because he was smart enough to know that Lee wasn't going to ever open herself up to him like this again.

"I guess this is goodbye."

"Yeah. But if you need help with this Steve guy let me know. I can keep an eye on him from the tower for you as well."

"Nah, I know you're busy," he said, plus it would be easier for him if he limited his contact with her. After the accident that had paralyzed his older brother, Aaron had vowed to never hurt anyone again.

It hadn't been an easy vow to keep and he'd done a good job at trying to destroy himself before he finally found the strength to acknowledge what he'd done and forgive himself. But today was the first time when he was almost tempted to ignore it.

To pretend he could have Lee and keep her safe. Physically, he knew he could, but emotionally…that was a different story. For him and for her.

She seemed to get him like no one else ever had and that scared him.

Aaron Quentin, who prided himself on being the biggest, baddest mofo in the room, was scared of what Lee could make him feel.

"How's it going?" Van asked in that gravelly voice of his when he walked into Lee's office later that afternoon.

"With the missing girl?"

"Yeah," he said as he turned a chair around at the conference table and sat down.

"Dead ends mostly. Her house was tossed, but to me, it looked like she'd cleared out before that happened. Her room was practically empty. Just found these two receipts in a left-behind jacket and this Polaroid," Lee said, tapping a key to open her evidence file so Van could get a look.

Her boss had always been a top investigator when they'd worked together for the government. She needed a second pair of eyes. And Van was the perfect man for the job. She'd taken some photos of the house as well, and she sat back in her chair while he took his time looking through them.

She'd spent the drive back to Price Tower pushing Aaron firmly out of her mind. There was something between them, but the two of them had jobs and being distracted could cost someone their life. That was something she wasn't willing to do.

"I've got a geotag on a club in West Hollywood on Isabell's phone, but Detective Monroe said that the phone was registered to the family, not just the girl. He's not going to investigate further unless they find a body or the family so he can question them."

"Well, time is money and the police force is stretched thin." Van scrutinized the items in the folder. "This receipt looks like it's from a food truck… Let me look around. It's familiar, so I might have grabbed lunch at it."

"Thanks. The instant photo and this one from her cloud account appear to have been taken in the same place. But she looks drastically different in both," Lee told him.

Van leaned in and switched between the two photos that Lee had directed him to. As he clicked between them, Lee watched Isabell's face go from a girl's to a woman's. It made her wonder if the high schooler had made a choice to leave and make her own way in the world. She'd be a runaway, but this other life might be better than what she had at home.

Lee was pretty sure it must be given that the girl had left and her parents hadn't reported her missing.

"Yeah, I think they are the same. You know where this place is?" Van asked.

"The geotag is that club I mentioned. Mistral's. Might go and check it out," she said.

"Good idea. If you find something and need backup, holler. I'm going to talk to a potential client tonight. Do you think you'd be able to do a two-week gig?" Van asked.

"Yeah. This is a side investigation," she said.

"But it's important too. I've been thinking of bringing on some more staff," Van added.

"I don't think we need it," she said with a shrug. But she suspected that was just her not wanting the team to change.

"Haven't made up my mind yet. We do have your new security team for the corporate client, which is a good revenue stream," her boss reminded her.

It was his subtle way of pointing out that things were already in flux. New team members would be added eventually. Lee knew from the past that waiting wasn't going to make it any easier for her to adjust to having unfamiliar people around. "I'm just being a hermit, I guess."

Van laughed. "But on the other hand, we got a good thing here."

"We do. But it's already changing. X is splitting his time between work and Florida to be with Obie. Luna's living at Nick's place."

"Yeah, but at least she's close and so is Kenji," he said. "Our profile is growing and I'm not sure I want to take on bigger clients, but there are some jobs I'm not sure I want to pass up either. I need your buy-in. We started this together."

They *had* started it together. Both of them pissed at their government bosses, who'd missed the fact that Cate O'Dell had been a double agent, and tired of seeing innocent people paying for big decisions that left collateral damage.

"We did, but you've always been the leader," Lee pointed out.

"And you the behind-the-scenes wizard who makes everything happen," Van said.

"Sometimes. You needed systems and that's where I shine. If we add more team members, would you bring them to the tower?" she asked. "We might need a second location."

"Or just leave that out of the employment contract," Van suggested. "I'm not sure what I'll find. We won't be hiring just *anyone*. It's important to get people who think like we do."

"I agree." For a moment, Aaron's face drifted through her mind. He was like-minded but not suited for bodyguard work. Maybe that was why she'd been afraid to take a chance on him that night in Miami. She knew that he was too much like her. Today had confirmed it.

They were both always going to put others first. Put *the job* first. They had to. She couldn't give in to lust or love or anything that would put innocent lives in jeopardy.

And she knew she was an all-or-nothing kind of woman. So when Aaron had told her he was the same, it hadn't really been a surprise. He was sort of the masculine version of herself. She knew better than anyone what that cost.

The fact that Mistral's was in West Hollywood wasn't surprising for Lee. She'd wanted to come during the day to scope the place out but hadn't been able to get free. And as she'd told Van earlier, this was her side gig. He had been contacted by a big corporate client who was thinking of hiring them for their internal security. Which was basically a new thing that Van was trying out, thanks to her suggestion.

She and Xander had worked together to write a proposal for a passive security system that would be monitored by a program that Lee had written. If they got this gig, Van would in fact have to follow through on his plan to hire a small staff that would work out of the client's building and report to her. From the moment they'd started Price Security, Lee hadn't exactly been in her element. She wasn't a bodyguard, though she was a sharpshooter, and was trained in hand-to-hand combat.

She knew that Van was doing this for her, to give her a chance to shine the way she'd helped him in the beginning, and she truly appreciated it. He'd even had her do the presentation, which she hadn't really liked, but everyone said she'd done good.

Getting changed back into her jeans and T-shirt with a flannel shirt over it had been the first thing she'd done after the meeting. And then, of course, she'd made sure the team were all set before heading out.

Once she left Wilshire and drove toward Mistral's, she wondered if she should have brought backup. But she was just going to ask a few questions to try to find the spot that Isabell had been in when she'd taken her selfie. Lee figured she'd be good.

She pulled into the parking lot and noticed that the club was at the end of a strip mall and most of the other shop fronts were dark and closed for the night. It was just about seven, so that made sense. She parked her car and, looking around, noticed that the club was a bit more upmarket than she'd expected.

Sitting in her car, she waited. She took a few pictures with the camera on her phone. A few minutes later, she got out and walked up to the club. It wasn't exactly empty but it wasn't crowded either. However, she knew she was early for the club crowd, and as she peered inside through the window, she didn't see any teenagers inside.

Or what *appeared* to be teenagers. Detective Miller had sent over the report that the officer had filed, and Mistral's had been ruled out as a location because they hadn't been able to verify that Isabell had been the sole user of her phone.

But in any case, Lee was here to see if the selfie had been taken in the club. To be accurate, she started at the far end of the mall, checking out the interiors of the shops, which wasn't too difficult as most had security lights on. She moved down the retail stores, getting to a coffee shop that was still open. She went in and the barista behind the counter informed her they were closed.

"No problem. Can I use the bathroom?"

"Okay," the barista said in an annoyed tone. "Just make it quick."

Lee made her way toward the facilities at the back and looked at Isabell's photo again. She was still trying to remotely crack the phone. Maybe then she'd be able to find other photos and where they were taken. She wanted to find something in the same time frame as the one the girl had posted.

The walls in the coffee shop didn't match the background, so she crossed this place off the list. She thanked the barista as she made her way out.

Her gut had said it was the nightclub, and now that was the only location left. Tucking her phone into her pocket, she strode back toward Mistral's. They didn't open until nine and Lee rapped on the door, which was opened by a bouncer.

"Sorry. Um… I'm looking for a job," she said.

He eyed her up and down. "Not sure you're qualified."

"Trust me, I am," she assured him.

"Flo is the one hiring. Go around the back. She might not let you in," the bouncer warned.

Of course, since in her casual T-shirt and jeans, she obviously didn't look like the ideal candidate. Lee debated leaving and coming back later, dressed for the club. But figured she'd give this a go first.

She walked around the side and immediately noticed that the brick wall in the background of Isabell's photo was very similar to the bricks here. She pulled her phone out and took a quick photo, not stopping as she kept going to the back door.

It opened outward toward her as she stepped up to it, knocking her back, and a strong hand grabbed her arm, steadying her. She glanced up into ice-blue eyes, her own going wide as she recognized Aaron.

He turned, pressing her between the building and his hard, muscular body. "What the hell are you doing here?"

"I'm here for information," she hissed.

"Fuck. I'm new here. You need to go."

Lee didn't have time to come up with a plan. She needed to get inside and didn't want to screw things up for Aaron. But she wasn't leaving. Since he was pressed against her, she just cupped his butt and said loudly, "You're the one who called me, babe."

"Quinn, this your chick?" someone asked.

He looked at her and could almost see him thinking things through.

"Yeah," she said, turning and tucking herself against his side.

Lee wasn't sure what being Aaron's chick involved or how she was going to get out of this, but for right now, it seemed to be her best way into the club.

Aaron tipped her head back up toward his and looked down hard into her eyes. She guessed this wasn't what he needed at the moment, but she wasn't going to let the chance to find Isabell slip away.

Chapter 6

Well, hell. That was all that Aaron was thinking as he dragged Lee into the club and into the office he'd just been given.

Steve left them alone, but Aaron hadn't swept the office yet, so he didn't know if it was safe. He wasn't happy with Lee. She was screwing up his job and wasn't she the computer geek? She should be at Price Tower and not at Mistral's, where he was on the trail of a drug kingpin.

Minor point, but she wasn't hot enough to be his undercover chick. Normally if he was paired with a partner undercover, it was a woman who had all eyes on her. Lee wasn't that. Sure, she was hot as hell and he hadn't been able to stop thinking about that kiss she'd dropped on him that had left him hard and wanting, but she wore jeans and a tee, neither were formfitting, and that flannel she threw on made her look like a biker babe from the '90s.

She didn't seem too happy with him either, but tough. He wasn't about to let her dictate whatever the hell this was.

Wait… Was Xander okay? Was she here because something had happened to his brother?

"I told you I'd see you at home," he growled as soon as they were in the nondescript office at the top of the stairs, over the bar. There was some music playing that could be heard through the floor, but it wasn't loud enough to mask their voices.

"Yeah, well, something came up that couldn't wait," she said carefully. Then mouthed, "I'm sorry."

"Is X okay?" he asked. He and his younger brother had just started talking again and the last thing Aaron wanted was for anything to happen to him.

"What? Yeah, he's fine. Sorry, it's, um, something else."

Which told him shit. "This *something else* couldn't wait? Jako wants me to impress these guys," Aaron said. Not that he expected she'd know who Jako was.

She bit her lower lip and nodded her head.

"I'll get you some other clothes if you're staying. I really have to prove myself here."

He pulled her close to him, dropping his head to whisper in her ear. "What are you doing here?"

"I'm looking for a girl who disappeared," she whispered back, wrapping her arms around his shoulders and shifting her body closer to his. "I'm guessing we're not alone."

He couldn't help but notice that Lee fit into his frame perfectly, her head at the same level as his shoulder. "I haven't had a chance to confirm."

"Okay. Sorry for this. Didn't know you'd be here. Could I look around and see if my girl was here?" she asked.

"No. Can't risk it," he said.

The door to the office opened and Steve walked in

with another man. He was the same height as Aaron but brawnier, and it was hard to tell if it was muscle or girth. Cocking his head to the side, he waited.

"You Quinn?"

Aaron nodded.

"Hector Ramos. I run this district. Who's that?"

Steve stepped forward and spoke before Aaron could. "His old lady. Bouncer said she's looking for work."

Aaron squeezed Lee's waist, hoping she'd get the message to keep her mouth shut. This was a complication he didn't need. Part of his success undercover was keeping things simple and uncomplicated. Nothing about the situation with Lee was simple.

"What do you do?" Ramos asked.

"I tend bar. Sorry for these clothes. I wasn't sure if Quinn was going to be able to get me a gig," she explained.

The other man looked her up and down, frowning with disapproval. "You got anything else to wear?"

"Yeah, of course."

"As long as Quinn is here, you can tend bar," he said.

"Thanks—"

"Quinn and I need to talk, so you go get changed and report to Flo," Ramos told her. "Steve will intro you."

Aaron felt his cover getting more out of his control. His partner wasn't going to be happy to hear about this. But at this point, Lee was now his woman and she was going to be working here.

She turned to Aaron, reached up and pulled his head toward hers. "I'm sorry," she repeated softly.

He was too, because she was stuck until he figured out how to get her out of this. He drew her closer, his hand on her ass, and kissed her hard. She pulled back and then followed Steve out of the office. Aaron crossed his arms over his chest and turned to Ramos.

"Jako mentioned this place needed a firm hand."

"It does. We run two operations out of here and the cops are checking up all the time. We can't afford sloppy management, and I don't do second chances," Ramos informed him. "You have two weeks to get this place in order."

"What's happening in two weeks?"

"That's your deadline, Quinn. Don't disappoint me. I've got two people who will be checking in with you and making drops. You let them know if anyone isn't pulling their weight. Even your woman. Don't let her take you down."

Quinn nodded. "Who are they?"

"Jorge and Diana. They'll stop by tonight to introduce themselves. Jako told you this place is different, right?"

"Yeah. Came straight from San Clemente. I've got some smarter clothes in my van," he said.

"Okay, then go get cleaned up and get ready for opening," Ramos said. "I'm sticking around tonight."

Great. But Aaron just nodded. "Be nice getting to know you."

Ramos just dismissed him. Aaron left the office and went down the stairs to find Lee getting shown the bar area. "Flo?"

"Yes."

"We have to go and get ready for opening. Can you show her the rest later?" he asked.

"Sure thing."

Lee walked to his side in that long, sexy stride of hers.

If this entire mission hadn't just gone FUBAR then he might appreciate the way she was blending in. *Might.* But that was something he was going to have to appreciate later.

She followed him out the back and to his van. Once they were inside, she started to talk but he shook his head. "Not until we are out of here."

Instead of driving to the apartment Jako had offered him, he headed to a safe house that the DEA had set up for him. It was a crappy apartment off West Hollywood. Lee stayed quiet, following him up the stairs to the first-floor apartment. Once she was inside and he'd closed the door behind him, he shook his head.

"What the actual hell?"

"Sorry," she said again. But really, at this point, so much of her recon mission had gotten away from her that she had no idea what to do next. "Like I said, I'm looking for a girl."

"And you think she was at Mistral's?"

"Yes. I tracked a photo she posted, but she's underage so…I'm not sure how she got in. Also the cops aren't certain if she shared the phone with someone else in her household, so I need to identify the background and the location to confirm she's been there."

"I really don't want you at the club. I'm just setting myself up with the gang," he said. "We can't take too long to confab. My partner should be here in a minute with a pizza so I can pass him the new setup info."

"How can I help?"

"You have to go back with me. So, what's your size and we'll get you a dress to wear behind the bar," he said.

"Clothes are really that big of a deal?"

"In the club they are. Also I'm sort of a player."

She arched a brow. *"Sort of?"*

He shook his head. "Yeah. Size?"

"Twelve and I have big hips," she said.

"They look okay to me," he said, letting his eyes drift down her body, sending the information to Denis, his partner.

"Is this a Price thing?"

"No, it's a favor for a friend," she said.

"That explains the lack of coordination. Normally you guys are top-notch."

Lee felt that. He was right—she should have made a solid plan. Part of it was she just wanted answers so she could close off the loop with Boyd and stop letting in those memories that he'd stirred up. The other part was that she was feeling the loss of Hannah and it made her want to do all the things she hadn't done for her friend.

"We are. I won't make this worse for you," she promised.

"We'll see. Ramos is going to be watching the club and the employees. So, as it turns out, we're going to have to ride out this couple thing after all. Can you do it?" he asked.

She wasn't entirely confident she could. She had her job at Price and she wasn't exactly great at relationships. "I have to talk to Van."

"Fine. Go ahead and do that. My contact is here."

Aaron left the apartment and Lee sank down on the couch, noticing it was very similar to the one in her apartment. She put her head in her hands for a minute and then took a deep breath.

This was an opportunity to really see what was going on at Mistral's, from the inside. But she was going to have to get clearance from Van. But even if she did, could she pull this off? It had been a long time since she'd been undercover. The last time had been with Van and Cate...and Cate had betrayed them. Van had changed while they'd been undercover, and she knew that it was difficult for anyone, herself included, to keep reality straight when you were living a lie 24-7.

She hit his number and he answered on the first ring.

"Lee," he said, his voice that warm, deep tone that made her smile. "How's my favorite girl?"

"Not sure she's going to be your fave for long. I was doing some legwork on my missing-girl case and crashed into Aaron's undercover op. I'm now his girlfriend and will be working at the bar..."

She heard the squeak of his chair as he leaned back in it and knew him well enough to know he was probably weighing all the options. "For how long?"

"I don't know. I can still work during the day," she said. "But I'll need my stuff brought to Aaron's apartment. He's talking to his partner. I'm not sure what the op will entail and if they will even clear me to stay."

"So the situation is fluid. You think the Montez girl was at the club?"

"Not one hundred, but everything is pointing that way."

"Keep me posted. I'll support you however I can," Van told her.

"Thanks."

Disconnecting the call, she leaned back against the couch and stared up at the ceiling. Her mind going a million miles a minute. *I can do this*, she kept telling herself. But at what cost?

Aaron walked back in with a duffel bag in one hand and a pizza box in the other. He tossed the box on the table. "Food and small comms devices in there. Clothes in here. What did Van say?"

"To keep him posted. I'm going to have to figure out how to work and do this," she said. "*If* I'm cleared to stay."

"Denis is checking with our boss. I don't think they'll like it, but you have undercover training and were an operative, so they'll probably clear it. However, they'll want me to get you out as quickly as I can."

"That works for me. I just need a quick look around and then we can orchestrate a big fight tonight," she said. "I'll storm out and that will be the end of it."

"Not tonight. I am meeting two lieutenants. I could use your eyes. You might pick up something I miss," he said.

"Okay. You got it. Different gangs?"

"We're not sure. Ramos said different operations, so it might be money houses and drug drops. I can't be certain. I was sent here because I helped clean house at Jako's."

"They are expecting you to do that again?"

"Yes, and I intend to." He crossed his arms over his chest and drilled his blue gaze into hers. "But, before we go any further, there's something you need to know..."

"What's that?"

"I'm not a super-nice guy undercover," he warned.

She shrugged. "I've been underground. I know nothing's real," she said.

"And yet *everything* is. You know that you can't fake anything. Be honest about everything in the lie so it seems more real."

Which wasn't an easy thing to do. She had always prided herself on her practicality, but she knew that being undercover made the world seem very different.

Aaron had to be at his office in the morning to talk to his boss. There was a lot of explaining he needed to do, and he got that. As upset as he was at seeing Lee, he knew the blame was solidly on him for putting her in this situation.

Reuniting with Xander meant that he had more connections in the US than he'd had before. Aaron had been uniquely suited to his undercover role because he was estranged from his family until now. Was he now more of a liability than an asset? He mulled it over as he changed in the living room while Lee used the bedroom to get ready.

Putting on a dress shirt that molded to his muscled arms, and then a pair of dark blue pants and a matching vest, he knew he looked sharp. He took a minute to make sure his hair was curling the way it was meant to and then decided to leave the stubble on his jaw because it made him look just the slightest bit like he was trying too hard.

One of the first things he'd learned about being undercover was that most of the time people saw what they wanted to. If he came off as someone who was willing to do anything to work his way up in the organization, then everyone would treat him that way.

Aaron sat down to put on his shoes. They were dress oxfords that had a knife in the tip of one toe. He'd had

them specially made after watching *Kingsman*. He liked
the idea of a hidden blade and had used it, well, zero
times, but there was also a chance he might get to.

He also had a small flesh-colored device that he put
behind his ear, which would record all of his conversa-
tions. It was activated by sound, so he couldn't turn it
on or off. His clothes were made of the latest-technology
cloth and were bulletproof. But his boss had wryly admitted probably more bullet *resistant*, so best not to get
shot at.

After bending down to put a small handgun in the
ankle holster he wore, he secured the large diamond in
his left ear. Then stood as Lee opened the bedroom door
and came out.

She wore a tank-style dress made out of the same
bulletproof material as his clothes. It hugged her curvy
frame, and until this moment, he had no idea how fit she
was. Her hips, which she'd warned him were ample, were
actually *perfect*, and his palms tingled thinking about
grabbing hold of them. In her jeans he hadn't realized
how hot she was. Which he really needed to forget because he was working.

It didn't matter that the scoop neck of the dress
showed her full breasts off or that her waist was tiny
and that all he could think about was sweeping her into
his arms and kissing her soundly.

But they were supposed to be acting like an ordinary
couple. He had to be able to touch her and not react. And
right now that wasn't possible. Maybe he should have
gone and gotten laid instead of visiting with his brother
before starting this job. Then maybe Lee wouldn't be

hitting all of his buttons and making it impossible for him to think about anything other than taking her to bed.

She arched both eyebrows at him. "You look like someone's version of a pimp."

"Ha. I like to dress nice and it's sort of my rep. You look good."

"Thanks. I hate clothes like this because I feel so exposed."

She kept one arm over her waist and he realized how different this was from her normal attire. "We can get you something else."

"No. They'll be expecting me in something like this, and it will make it easier for me to remember this is all pretend."

She had a point. "Speaking of that, you were good earlier with the close touches. If you get in a jam, you come and grab me."

She nodded. He walked over to her, pushing her silky brown hair aside, and put the small gadget, just like his, behind her ear. "This is a listening device. Just speak and backup will raid the place and get you out."

"Won't that set you back?"

"Your safety is more important. We can always rebuild. I'm new to this area so won't be connected to any raids, but you…" He shot her a stern look. "Don't mess around if you feel you're in danger."

"I won't. I didn't bring a weapon because I was just doing recon but—"

"That's fine. I don't want you armed. But once we see the setup, there might be a chance to put one behind the bar. Just in case you need it."

She nodded silently, waiting for him to continue.

"As you know from Ramos, I'm called Quinn. That's it—just one name. I came from London and work in the Hollywood scene. And as for how I rose up the ranks… I saw something that wasn't right in Jako's organization and alerted him to a mole from another gang, which he took care of." He cleared his throat. "They know your first name is Lee. I'd stick with something hard to trace like Smith or Jones for a family name if you're pushed. But normally, that's not an issue."

"Okay. Quinn. Got it." She pursed her lips. "And what about us? How'd I end up as your old lady?"

He didn't miss a beat. "We've been working together since I got to LA. You were tending bar at a club where I was employed, we hooked up and have been a team since."

"Love it." She smirked. "Tomorrow I'll build an on-line presence for us and get some IDs. Are we staying here?"

"We'll be here at night, but you can go back to Price Tower during the day," he told her. "The situation is fluid until I figure out what's going on at Mistral's and you get what you need for your missing girl."

Chapter 7

Aaron's partner was going to be nearby, and Lee suspected that Van wasn't too far away either. She'd tapped into the feed that the DEA device had and sent a signal back to her computer at Price Tower. Then she sent a text with the link to Van.

He'd just thumbed-up the message.

Lee was the first to admit that things weren't the best. But whenever she was forced back into her adolescence with Boyd and Hannah, they never were. The past wasn't a place she wanted to be, so she shook the memories off and turned to Aaron, watching the streetlights illuminate his face as he drove.

He and Xander had similar features, but there was something different about Aaron. A rougher edge than Xander had. Probably because of working undercover, she supposed. "In case it comes up, when did you get to LA? And also…where in the UK are you from?"

He gave a sort of nod and she watched as his accent and body language started to change. Watching him shift into Quinn was interesting.

"Six months ago, babe. I am originally from East London but had been living and working in North

London—Finchley," he said. "We met my first night here. It was instant connection and you couldn't resist my charm."

She arched one eyebrow at him but realized he couldn't see her. "You *thought* I couldn't, but you did have charisma, and even though I saw through your practiced moves, I let you buy me a drink at the end of the night."

He turned to look over at her. "I liked that you saw through me, and even though I needed to get myself established, you and I hooked up."

"Am I aware you deal drugs?" she asked.

"All you know is that I do something that involves me moving around and being out of our apartment all day and night. You were working at a different bar... The specifics are up to you," he said.

Lee pulled her smartphone out of her pocket. "Let me set that up in case they check."

She sent a quick text to Nicholas DeVere, billionaire business and nightclub owner and also the husband of her bestie Luna. He was down to have his staff vouch for her. "Done. We met at Madness, and I was working as a bartender there. I left because they banned you."

"Good. That works. I guess they were suspicious of what I was doing," Aaron said.

"Definitely." She shot him a worried look. "I don't want Nick caught up in this," she said.

"Me either," he said as he pulled into a parking spot at the strip mall. "I'm not sure what we're going into. It's nothing I can't handle, but like I said, if you get scared just say the word and the DEA will raid—"

"I'm not going to get scared. You know I've worked undercover before," she said.

"But you got out," he said pointedly.

"I did," she admitted. "It's not my favorite gig, but I want to find this girl. And the cops aren't going to start looking unless they have some evidence that she was somewhere she wasn't supposed to be."

"Fair enough." Abruptly he shifted around, his hand on her face, his eyes more serious than she'd ever seen them. "Stay safe."

"I will. You too," she murmured.

He parked his van off to the side, and after they got out, she pulled the ponytail from her hair and shook her head, feeling the weight of her long hair fall around her shoulders. It was June in LA, so the heat of the day had sort of disappeared, but it wasn't chilly. It had been years since she'd worn heels but that first step shifted something inside of her.

Her hips sort of fell into a different rhythm as she stretched her stride to keep up with Aaron. He stopped and watched her walking, shaking his head and letting out a wolf whistle. He put his hand on her butt and leaned in, kissing her but also whispering against her mouth.

"Last chance to walk away," he said.

She nipped his lower lip. "Stop trying to make me leave."

He straightened and turned, keeping his hand on the small of her back as they approached the club. The bouncer nodded at them as they strode past the queue of people waiting, dropping the rope and letting them in.

Her stomach was a riot of butterflies and as much as she'd reassured Aaron she was ready for this, she knew that she wasn't. She'd been at her desk for more than a decade. Fieldwork required a lot more than just knowledge and nerves. It required her to really reach deep and be someone she hadn't been in a long time.

A woman she wasn't sure she liked but one that she knew she had to be if she was going to find Isabell.

She headed to the bar and Aaron just nodded at her as he headed toward the stairs and whatever it was he was going to do. Flo gave her a welcome look.

"We're slammed, hon. Get to work and I'll show you the rest of the setup when we have a lull."

Lee started taking orders and there was a moment where her memories of Grandpa's place flooded back. He wasn't just her comfort at night when she couldn't sleep. He'd taught her how to tend bar, make drinks and observe people. He'd been the biggest influence on the woman she was today, and she knew she'd done him a disservice by trying to leave all of that behind.

"Do we ID?" she asked, noticing some customers who looked questionable.

"We do early in the night but stop around ten," Flo said.

"Cool."

This was the first chink in the no-minors policy she'd seen. And the time stamp on Isabell's photos had been 11:30 p.m. She tucked that information away and started taking orders and making drinks. Flo handled the register since Lee hadn't been trained, but making drinks was pretty easy.

As the night went on, she noticed a number of customers disappearing down the hall toward the bathroom and then coming back with a different energy. Another tidbit she filed away.

* * *

Ramos was still in the office and there were two other dudes with him when Aaron walked in. They didn't have the polish of what he expected from the two people that Ramos had mentioned earlier.

One of them had gang tats around his neck. Aaron hadn't been on the West Coast long enough to ID them, but he was pretty sure he'd seen them in the dossier he'd been given when he landed. The guy also had the word *pain* tattooed on his knuckles.

"Quinn, these two will report to you. Pain and Panic work Mistral's and two more clubs in the area. They'll pick up from you at the beginning of the night and pay out at the end."

"Pain and Panic?"

"Yeah, we liked Hercules as kids and it sort of suits us," Panic said.

Aaron watched as a safe built into one wall was opened and the men were given their take for the night. Both of them left a few minutes later and the safe was closed. Ramos gave him the combination to the lock and told him that his second-in-command, Jorge, would come by every morning at nine to collect the money.

There were a few more housekeeping things. Mainly that he was the one responsible for the take at Mistral's, and if there were any discrepancies, Aaron would be responsible for sorting them out before Jorge came by for the money.

"Jorge will give you more info on that when he gets here. Diana has been running out of the club for the last three months. Her operation is different and you don't do anything but make sure that the room down the hall is kept locked. Her people move in and out throughout the night, and they do their pickup at noon," Ramos told him.

"What are they picking up?"

"You don't need to know. Flo cleans the room after they leave," Ramos said. "You just make sure that door stays locked and no one goes in or out. Got it?"

"Got it," Aaron replied, spreading his hands out. "Do I stay up here or down on the floor?"

"Normally you'd be downstairs. You're in charge of Mistral's, so keep your eye out for plants and make sure no one makes trouble. We don't need the cops called for drunk and disorderly."

Aaron cracked his knuckles. "I can take care of anything that comes up."

"That's what I like to hear," Ramos said. "Jako speaks highly of you."

Aaron nodded. He wasn't sure how to respond to that. "That's good of him."

"It is. He's also put his neck out for you."

There was a knock at the door before Ramos could say anything else. He called out for them to enter. A man walked in first who was definitely Ramos's second-in-command. He wore the wealth he'd made off the streets like a big, gaudy badge. Thick gold chains wound around his neck and a diamond as big as Aaron's pinky glimmered in his ear. His head was shaved, and when he smiled, he flashed a gold tooth. He greeted Ramos like a brother and then turned to look Aaron over.

From the looks of it, this guy was a fighter and used to being the alpha, something that Aaron always saw as a challenge. It was probably why he'd been so good at working his way up organizations when he was under-cover. That Quentin boy in him wasn't going to settle for second place, even when he was undercover.

"Jorge, this is Quinn. He's going to be running Mistral's," Ramos said.

Jorge held his hand out, and when Aaron took it, the other man squeezed hard. He returned the favor, not letting up until Jorge sort of grunted and let go. "You won't deal with me unless there's a problem."

"Then, I hope that won't happen," Aaron retorted.

"Agreed. Diana here yet?"

"No. She should be," Ramos answered. "Want a drink?"

"Tequila on the rocks," Jorge said.

Ramos looked over at Aaron and he just nodded. "Same."

Retrieving his phone, Ramos called down and placed the order just as the door opened and a woman walked in. She was tall, dressed all in black and had gorgeous red hair that hung around her shoulders. She wore a similar-style dress to the one Lee had put on. But that was where the similarity ended.

This woman carried herself as if she were on a runway. She commanded attention and knew it. All eyes were on her and he had the feeling that was exactly what she wanted.

"Diana."

"Ramos. This the new guy?"

"Quinn," Aaron said, going over to her.

She gave him a shrewd glance, her gaze moving over his body and then coming back to meet his eyes. The

way she searched his face, Aaron knew she was prob-
ing to see if he was what he said.

He just held that stare and then gave her a slight smile.
"Like what you see?"

"A Brit?"

"Yes," he replied, lifting both his eyebrows. "Do you
like my accent?"

"It'll do and so will you for now," she said. "Were
you told to stay out of my way?"

Aaron nodded. Still not sure what it was she was in
charge of. There was a knock at the door and he heard
Lee's voice saying "drinks."

Ramos nodded at him to go and get them. He went to
open the door and took the tray from her. Making sure
she didn't enter the room. He had a feeling that Ramos
didn't want her in here, and whatever was going on, it felt
tenser than it had when only he and Jorge had been there.

The redhead was beautiful, but there was something
dangerous about her. Whereas with Jorge he'd felt that
stir of fighting to be alpha, Diana was something else
and Aaron wasn't sure what yet.

One thing he knew for sure—he wanted Lee as far
away from this as he could get her. Something he was
pretty damned sure she wouldn't agree to.

Aaron took the drinks from her, and Lee glanced over
his shoulder as she started to turn away, but did a double
take when she recognized the woman. She tried to turn
back, but Aaron put his hand on her hip and pushed her
toward the stairs, stepping back into the room and closing the door firmly.

Lee stopped on the stairs, trying to process what she'd

just seen. *Cate O'Dell*. The woman who'd betrayed her and Van on their last mission for the government and nearly cost Van his life and his reputation.

Lee couldn't believe she was here. Maybe she'd been mistaken. She had to be careful because Cate would recognize her. Nerves roiling through her, she hurried back down the stairs. Could she be jumping to a conclusion here? Well, until she saw the woman again, she couldn't be sure.

She went back behind the bar but kept her eye on the stairs. There was only one way down, so Cate would have to take them.

She mixed drinks and joked with customers, but she couldn't concentrate. Cate shouldn't be here. She'd been revealed to be a top lieutenant in an international crime syndicate that Lee knew still operated. But Cate had been rumored to have been killed at the Mexican border nearly four years ago.

"You can take a break if you want," Flo said.

"Thanks."

Lee grabbed her bag and went down the hall toward the bathroom. She took her phone out, pretending to use the camera to check her makeup but really checked out Isabell's selfie. Then Lee lifted her phone and took a photo of herself with the wall behind her.

She'd analyze it later. She turned to walk away from the bathroom since the line wasn't moving and she'd got what she'd come down there for. But she halted when she noticed someone coming down the stairs. It wasn't the red-haired woman but, instead, a big man who noticed her watching him and flashed her a big grin. She smiled back before heading behind the bar. Her heart was racing and she really wasn't sure she could remember anything.

But the familiar sounds and smells of the bar comforted her as they always had. Making Jägerbombs for a group of college-age kids was what she needed to start feeling normal again.

She could almost convince herself that she'd imagined Cate. That was probably the case. She forced herself to concentrate on tending bar and not let her anxiety get the better of her.

She was pouring shots of tequila for a group a little while later when she noticed movement out of the corner of her eye. Aaron came down and the woman was behind him. Lee kept her head lowered so that her hair fell forward to block her own features but she could still watch.

As the redhead said something to Aaron, Lee got a good look at her and the blood in her veins went cold.

Cate O'Dell was definitely alive.

"Whoa, we don't overpour!" Flo reprimanded.

"Sorry." Lee lifted the bottle and then took a deep breath. "I'll pay for that."

"You will. Don't let it happen again."

Hands shaking, she put the bottle back on the shelf and then turned, but Cate was gone. Aaron was working the club, moving through the customers, and Lee turned to face the rear of the bar. What was she going to do?

Van was wrecked after Cate had betrayed them. Like, broken in a way she'd never seen him before. Which meant she wasn't going to be able to take this back to the team. She was going to have to handle this herself.

Immediately she started to concoct a plan to distance

herself from Price until she could take Cate down. Get that traitor locked up where she couldn't hurt Van again.

Because that woman had been Van's Achilles' heel. The one weakness in a man who seemingly had none.

Fitting that her boss's weakness should be in play at the same time that hers was. She was here trying to make up for losing Hannah, on a mission to find and save Isabell for Boyd, who had also lost Hannah.

It wasn't going to bring their friend back, or make either of them feel better, but they both had to keep doing this. Had to keep trying to watch out for the innocent. Now she had a second goal.

Keep Van safe.

He'd rebuilt his life and his career with Price Security. He was respected again and Lee knew that her friend was stronger because of everything he'd survived. Lee had always believed she was too, but there was a part of her that wondered if she truly was.

Her body's reaction to seeing Cate told her there was still unresolved issues from the past. She might like to say she was a no-regrets kind of woman but deep down she knew the truth.

She *had* regrets.

Trusting Cate, letting her in and believing that she could have a genuine friendship with someone while undercover had been a mistake. She'd missed things she should have seen because she'd started to believe the lie they were living.

It was doubly important she didn't do that this time around. Didn't allow herself to see Aaron as anything other than a coworker. No matter how powerfully drawn they were to one another or how much she saw the humor under his flirty facade. She had to keep her guard up. She had to remember that Aaron was simply playing a role.

That what they were feeling wasn't *real*.

And besides…she had cast herself into his undercover mission. He had made it clear that he didn't want her there and he'd do what he had to in order to shut down the drug operation running out of this club.

He wasn't her friend and he wasn't someone she could lean on. Even if she wanted to.

Bottom line? She was in this on her own. Finding Isabell was still her main focus, but now bringing down Cate and ensuring that Van never found out she was alive was her second.

Chapter 8

Lee was pissed at herself for getting distracted by this bombshell over Cate O'Dell. Aaron was on the floor, and she thought she'd seen Denis a few minutes ago but he looked more like a party dude than he had earlier in the day.

Flo was watching her, so Lee knew she needed to get her shit together. Cate wasn't a bit player. Whatever was going on in Mistral's...if she was here, then this was big. Her mind was racing as she made a tray of shots to take to the VIP booth in the back.

Was Van in danger? Was *she*? Why was Cate back in LA after having been reported deceased? Lee really hated this role she'd been forced into, because she wanted to be at her computer. Fingers moving over the keyboard so she could confirm once and for all that the woman she'd glimpsed was from Lee's own past and not just another ghost who was dogging her.

Hannah's ghost had been there since the moment she'd taken that damned meeting with Boyd. The past had been stirred up and nothing she did, no matter how many programs she wrote or algorithms she created, was going to give her an answer that would put it to bed forever.

She knew that.

Aaron glanced over at her and lifted both eyebrows, but she just gave him a tight smile. That was all the re-assurance that she could muster for him at the moment. She was dealing with her own stuff and it was taking all she had to stay in the role.

She *had* to. Aaron's life depended on it. If she went after Cate, she could blow his cover. The chances of the other woman recognizing her were high, Lee knew that. She was no closer to finding Isabell and this gamble to try to discover if the club played a part in her disappearance hadn't paid off so far.

Cate was part of La Fortunata crime family. Though no one in the government had been aware of it at the time, she'd hidden her connection during her recruitment and training. She'd been a plant from the beginning. And Lee and Van had teamed up with her, thinking she was like them. Someone who had wanted to change the world.

Idealistic and young, they'd bonded into a tight three-some who worked their way through assignments and racked up praise and wins. Wins had been so important to Lee back in the day. That might have been part of the reason she'd kept quiet when she realized that Van and Cate were having an affair.

Even though every bit of training they'd had warned them not to get involved during undercover work. Except Lee had thought the bosses must be wrong because that relationship had been leading them deeper and deeper

into the underbelly of one of the largest crime syndicates in the world.

Until it wasn't.

"Hey, your man's watching you. Take the shots to the
VIP room, see what he wants and then get back here,"
Flo said, breaking into her thoughts.

Lee nodded. Taking the tray, she slowly made her
way through the throngs of people dancing and hooking up in the club. It was hot in here and Lee shook her
head as she skimmed the crowd. The woman was gone.
She wasn't going to see anyone else from her past in this
room. She knew that.

But it felt like every instinct she had was overstimu-
lated, and now she wasn't sure of herself. The bouncer
for the VIP section let her pass and she took the shots
to a table of twentysomethings that had been splashing
cash all night. They had a group of women with them
now and Lee searched their faces, looking for Isabell,
but the girl wasn't there.

So even if the hallway leading to the bathroom was
where she'd been, there was no sign of her at this table.
She served the shots and then walked out of the VIP section. But Aaron was waiting for her, taking her wrist and
turning her so she was pinned between him and the wall.

His move blocked her from the room and he kept a
distance between their bodies. "You okay?" he whispered.

"Yeah. Sorry for trying to get in earlier. I thought the
woman looked familiar."

"We can discuss it later." His blue gaze captured hers.
"Do I need to get you out?"

"How?"

"Like you said earlier. We orchestrate a big fight and you're gone," he said.

She thought about it. But that would be taking the easy way out. Plus, if her instincts were correct and that woman was in fact Cate, Lee wanted to stay close to her to find out what she was up to. It was just that she'd been reported and confirmed deceased. Lee always trusted her gut, and right now, it was saying that Cate O'Dell was not dead. "I'm good."

Aaron lifted his hand and touched her face. "Would she recognize you?"

"I don't know," she said honestly. She'd changed a lot from the woman she'd been at twenty. Her hair had darkened over the decades and Lee's body had become rounder and more *adult*, for lack of a better word.

Aaron took a deep breath. "We'll let this ride for now."

"Yeah," she said.

"Back to work then," he ordered, turning and smacking her ass as she walked away.

It wasn't a move she would have expected from Aaron, but she guessed this was more *Quinn*. Van always said, when working undercover, to keep the parts of yourself that were at your core but to create another version. Lee had sucked at it back then, and given how she was feeling tonight, was pretty sure that hadn't changed.

What she wanted was to have never come to this club. Then she wouldn't be Aaron's pretend lover, she wouldn't have seen Cate and…she wouldn't be closer to finding Isabell. Because one of the things that La Fortunata crime syndicate ran was a very lucrative and prolific human trafficking network.

Lee found herself hoping that Isabell was a runaway

in a bad situation, and not a victim of La Fortunata, because if they had her, it was going to take more than research and knowledge to set her free.

The rest of the evening was uneventful, and when it was time to go, Lee followed him back to his apartment since she'd left her car at Mistral's earlier. Aaron was worried about the unknowns on this mission. Denis had followed a group out of the club and was still tracking down that lead. Aaron debated telling his partner that Lee might have a connection to the woman. But they hadn't had a debrief yet and so much information was still in flux.

He parked the van and then waited for Lee to get out of her Dodge. The day had been hard for her and it was written all over her lovely face. He had to find a way to get her out of this undercover gig. No matter that she was smart and capable and had worked undercover for the government, this wasn't an easy job and not everyone thrived in it the way Aaron did.

He also was distracted by her. Tonight he should have been working the club and figuring out who the regulars were. He was concerned about the Chacals because it was clear there was something more going on with the rival gang. But then he'd seen Lee looking—*lost* wasn't the right word but something pretty damned close—and he'd had to check on her.

She came up next to him now, putting her arm around his hips as they walked up to his apartment. She smelled of booze and the club and when she dropped her arm as he unlocked the apartment and opened the door, she smacked him on the butt as she walked in.

He had to smile because he'd suspected that she'd be offended by his ass tap earlier. But he hadn't been able to resist. He'd determined to keep a physical distance between them, and while he'd worked undercover with another female operative as a "couple" in the past and kept it strictly platonic, this was Lee and he wanted her. *Badly.*

"Guess you're not a fan of that," he quipped as he closed the door behind him.

His apartment had been set up with silent alarms and he knew no one had been in there since they'd left.

"No. But I get that Quinn is."

He grinned. "Yeah. I have to be sort of smarmy as Quinn." He undid his tie and the buttons on his vest. Then, shrugging out of the vest, he hung it on the back of a chair. He leaned against the breakfast bar, watching as Lee took off her shoes before sitting down.

"Catch me up on your investigation. Do you think the girl was at Mistral's?" he asked. Work was the only thing he was going to think about tonight. Not how long her legs looked under that slip dress she wore or how, when she had her hair down, she looked softer, *sexier* than she had before.

"Actually, I think she might have been. Not that that is going to help me find her," Lee said, standing back up and coming over to him with a photo that she'd pulled up on her phone. "This is the one I snapped in the hall leading to the bathroom at the club." She swiped to a second image. "And if you compare it to the brick wall from this Polaroid I found in what I assume to be her bedroom...it's the same." She sighed. "Of course, right now, I know it's circumstantial and not solid."

He took her phone and their fingers brushed, sending a tingle up his arm. Which he ignored, concentrating on the photos on her phone instead.

The background did look similar, and he studied the girl's face but couldn't recall seeing anyone who looked like her tonight. "I'll keep my eye out for her."

"Thanks. What about your investigation? Any new developments?" she asked.

He turned toward her. "We're not done with you yet. The woman. Who is she?"

"Well, first off she's supposed to be dead." Lee sighed. "But before we get into it...do you have anything to drink?"

"A couple of Coronas and water," he said. "Sorry, just got back here."

"Corona would be nice," she said.

"Go sit down and I'll grab them."

She went to the couch, curling her leg underneath and sitting in the corner against the armrest. Rubbing the back of her neck, she rotated her head and then tipped it back for a moment. He opened the beers and walked over, handing her one before sitting down in the arm-chair across from her.

"So she's *supposed* to be dead...?"

This was knowledge he needed so he could figure out what to do with Lee. Already his mission had changed because of her appearance, and now she might be putting his investigation at risk. He and Denis had done months of work before he'd come out here and gone undercover. That was something he wasn't going to sacrifice.

Not even for her.

"Yeah. So she looks like Cate O'Dell, but she had

other names and aliases. She was part of La Fortunata crime syndicate. She used an assumed name to get into the FBI where she worked with myself and Van."

"What happened?"

"She betrayed us. Almost got us killed and then escaped before she could be arrested. I've kept tabs on her but, four years ago, got word she'd been killed in Mexico."

Aaron took a sip of his beer, draining half of it in one long gulp. He couldn't help noticing that Lee just held her bottle, rolling it between her palms and switching it from hand to hand but not drinking.

"And tonight?" he asked. He felt like he was interrogating a subject. Lee was hiding something, giving just bare-bones answers to every question he asked. He couldn't allow secrets in this apartment; this part of the relationship had to be real and honest.

"I don't know. She looks like Cate and everything inside of me is telling me it's her. But I need proof." She blew out a breath. "I want to get back to Price Tower and start searching security footage to confirm that she's still alive," she said.

"Okay. Do that and let me know the minute you find anything." He turned to her and muttered, "But fair warning—we've danced around La Fortunata crime family for years and they are a tough nut to crack. My boss figures they are made up of different smaller groups and so getting to the top is almost impossible," Aaron said.

"I will. If it is in fact Cate…I don't want Van to know. She almost killed him," Lee said.

"If it is, then this entire op just leveled up."

* * *

Lee was tired *and* wired and wanted to be at her computer, but she also didn't really want to leave Aaron. He was pulling information from her with an innate skill that she wouldn't have expected from him. Which was definitely her bad. She'd just seen the muscles, those blue eyes and his charming smile and figured he didn't have a subtle bone in his body, but she was starting to see more.

She wondered if his bosses at the DEA were aware of it but figured they had to be. That was probably why they were taking him from the East Coast to the West Coast instead of pulling him out of undercover work. He had been good at changing to fit his environment as well, which should have made her a little bit wary of him. But instead it just intrigued her and made her want him more.

There was so much to unpack on this case, and if she could give the DEA a lead to La Fortunata, then she knew that Aaron would take it. But he might have to burn her to do it. Being a liability to him and creating risk to him and Denis wasn't something Lee wanted, but she knew the possibility was there.

"I'll pull what I have and send it to you," she said. "Okay, your turn now. How's your op?"

"Interesting. I was a bagman in San Clemente, but up here, they have me overseeing drops and just making sure what comes in stays in. Might have something that could help with your missing girl."

She leaned toward him, intrigued. "How so?"

"Well, the redheaded woman, whose name is 'Diana,' has a room that is kept locked and that no one is allowed in except at 10:00 a.m. to clean it. Sounds to me like human trafficking, which I'll be including in my report to my boss. That means that FBI will probably be getting involved."

"And I'll duck out if that's the case but still keep trying to find Isabell. Actually, that makes sense if the woman is Cate. Human trafficking was what we had been investigating when she burned us and left us for dead."

"Do you have a contact still at the agency?"

"I do," she admitted. Not that she wanted to reach out, but she would. "Want me to see what they know?"

"Yes. Are you working tomorrow at Mistral's?" he asked.

"Yeah. The next three nights. Eight to two."

"I'll be at the club in the morning to see who comes in and out," he said. "I'm meant to watch the pickups and make sure nothing goes wrong. Denis will be doing surveillance, so if you want to get a less conspicuous car, maybe you can follow them when they leave."

"Will Diana be back to do the pickup?" Lee asked.

"Doubtful. If it's people then they'll be moved in a van or larger truck. Denis is going to follow the drug money, and until we get in touch with the FBI task force, the human trafficking won't be tracked."

"Yeah, I can do it." She rolled the beer bottle between her hands again. Tonight she'd felt wild and not in control, but tomorrow she would be. Well, later today, since it was nearly 3:00 a.m. She still had work to do back at Price Tower for her day job and this investigation.

"I need to head home if I'm going to get started on this," she said.

"That's fine. Be back here by 8:00 a.m. Can I ask you a personal question?"

"Yes."

"Why ask for the beer?"

"Oh… I thought it would make you more at ease," she said. She didn't drink very often for a number of reasons. It would be easy to point to her addicted parents and use that as an excuse, but the truth was she had drunk a lot in college and hated how out of control it made her feel. It had warped her senses and made it hard to remember what was real.

"I'm always chill," he said.

She lifted both eyebrows. "I thought we had honesty in this room."

He laughed and reached over to take the beer she'd put on the coffee table. He took a swallow and then sort of nodded. "Fair enough. I'm not always chill, but I don't need a drink to put me at ease."

She could see that about him. He was very good at controlling himself and letting others see just what he wanted them to see. There were a few glimpses of the man she'd kissed, the man she'd drunk tequila with in Miami. That man tempted her and would be a welcome break from the tension riding her harder than any case had since Cate O'Dell had betrayed her.

She saw a competent agent in this apartment, someone who was more intelligent than she had guessed, and savvy at knowing how the gang he was infiltrating worked.

"Just seemed like an icebreaker, and in case you haven't noticed it yet, I'm awkward when I'm not behind my keyboard."

"You're not awkward at all," he said. "Or at least not around me."

He leaned forward as he finished her beer and put the bottle back on the table. "I think that's my signal to tell you good night."

She almost asked why, but she knew. The tension between them was palpable. It had been a long day and falling into his arms and into his bed would be a nice stress reliever, if it wouldn't create more problems. She stood up and got her belongings from earlier and just nodded at him.

"Good night."

Chapter 9

It felt like it had been months since she'd been back at her place, instead of just a day. The map she'd spread out on the table still sat there as well as a note from Van that just had a smiley face on it.

What was she going to do? He'd been in here telling her to make sure the CIA understood that Kenji wasn't available for any work and yet Lee was going to have to make contact with their old boss at the FBI and the human trafficking unit. She rubbed her neck as she stood in the middle of the room. She had a lot to do before 8:00 a.m. and honestly was wrecked. It had been a long day; she was going to try to get a solid four hours before she had to be back to trail the woman who she believed to be Cate.

She checked her computers for results and they still had nothing. This missing girl had opened a breach to her past that Lee didn't want to deal with. There had never been anything tying Hannah's disappearance to human trafficking; in fact, there had been nothing in all these years. Just that one kid who'd seen her get into a gray Jeep Cherokee and that was it. Nothing ever again.

No body, no ransom notes, no sign of the girl that had

been her best friend. Her stomach ached at the thought of Isabell Montez having the same fate. And a part of her knew she was reaching when she tried to tie Isabell to human trafficking. But it was an explanation.

She'd meant to go to bed, but instead grabbed a Red Bull from the fridge and pulled up a program that analyzed backgrounds in photos to identify the location. Specifically, those two photos. The one she'd taken tonight and the one of the Polaroid that Isabell had taken were scanned in. She took a sip of the Red Bull and grimaced, not really liking the taste, and realized that it wasn't working anyway.

She was exhausted and no amount of caffeine was going to help.

Yawning, she glanced down at her phone and saw it was already 5:00 a.m. She had a lot of work left to do here and wasn't going to be able to get back to Aaron in two hours, no matter how much she wanted to. Leaning forward, she put her head on her desk. Never had she felt this out of control. Facts and information were power and she always made sure she had them both at her fingertips.

But this time her facts were leading her to the past and she wasn't sure if it was just what she wanted to find or actual truth in the information.

There was a knock on the office door before it opened and Rick Stone walked in. The former DEA agent worked for Price Security. He gave off a big, soft puppy-dog kind of vibe. His thick blond hair was tousled as always and he had on jeans and a button-down. "Hey. Van mentioned you were pulling an all-nighter and might need a hand."

Van once again was two steps ahead of her. Which

she appreciated as always. Trusting in others had always been hard for her, but with her friend, he just was there. All the time.

"Are you free today?"

"Until four this afternoon, when I'm working. What do you need?"

Was she really going to send him in her place? She didn't want to but didn't have much choice in the matter. "I'm meant to meet Aaron Quentin and his partner, Denis, to do some surveillance. Could you take it?"

"Sure. What's the situation?"

She quickly filled him in, and since Rick was former DEA, he had contacts in the local office and sent a text getting approval from Denis and Aaron to take her place. She kept the fact that the woman might be someone from her and Van's past quiet.

"If you can get clear photos of all the players, I'd appreciate that," she said.

"I'll do my best. So, how did you stumble into this?" Rick asked. "I thought you were looking for a missing girl."

"I am. She was at that club and I'm trying to prove it so I can get the detective assigned to her case to really start looking for her," Lee explained. "My gut is telling me that she's in danger, but so far, the evidence isn't showing much. Her home was broken into and tossed, but it seemed as if the girl left before that."

"So were they searching for the parents or the girl?" Rick furrowed his brow. "Who brought the trouble to the house?"

Her colleague's questions were good ones that Lee

knew she had to find answers to. "Not sure. How do I find out?"

"I'd start with arrests. Do you know the parents' names? Why haven't the cops checked with them?"

"They did. They've been gone, and no one has seen them or their car. It's like they disappeared into thin air," Lee said. Just like Hannah. Except that no one just disappeared without a reason. She had to start compiling a better picture of who Isabell Montez was.

Which meant she was going to have to go back to Boyd and maybe to the high school he taught at to ask about her.

"Well, in that case, start with what you know and go from there."

"Will do. Thanks, Rick, for the advice…and for helping me out," she said. "There's Fanta in the fridge if you want some."

"Appreciate it. I haven't had breakfast yet. I'll grab one and head over to Mistral's. They said the FBI is sending over someone too from human trafficking," he mentioned as he walked to the fridge. "I'll get as much as I can from them."

"I'm going to reach out to my contact at the FBI as well," Lee told him. "If the girl was taken then this changes things."

"It does. And it definitely raises the question about what really happened to the rest of her family," Rick said.

"I'm going to try to narrow that down today. I need a few hours of sleep first though…"

"That's what Van thought. You sleep and do your magic with the computer and I'll report back," Rick said, waving as he strode out the door.

* * *

Aaron had talked to Rick Stone in Miami when his brother had helped him out taking down the La Familia Sanchez crime gang. The former DEA agent was quiet but efficient and easy to get along with. In a way, he reminded Aaron of Denis. The two men were sitting in their respective cars on opposite sides of the parking lot, both of them seeming to be asleep in their vehicles.

He walked into the club, his hair still a little wet from the shower. Sleep was always a luxury when he was on an op but Lee was making it even harder to crash. All he'd been able to think about was her in the bed next to him.

It was quiet but smelled of booze as he walked through. He closed the door behind him and heard the voices at the top of the stairs. The money was all in a safe in the office that Ramos had given him. Aaron now had the code, but no one else did.

Last night before he left, he'd stored the bags of money in there. He knew that a shipment of "goods" was meant to arrive after lunch at a location that Aaron hadn't been informed of. And he was pretty sure that Ramos was checking to make sure he wasn't a snitch. Seeing Steve yesterday made Aaron edgy. He didn't know what was going on, and after all the research he and Denis had done before getting here, it seemed there was still a lot they didn't know.

Jorge was waiting at the top of the stairs with another man Aaron didn't recognize. They both straightened from the wall when Aaron walked up.

"Was about to call Ramos."

"Why?" Aaron asked.

"Thought you'd skipped out with the money," Jorge said.

"No. Just not a morning man." Before unlocking the door and going into the office, Aaron gestured toward the other dude. "Who's this?"

"Palmer. Somedays it might just be him or me. We're the only two authorized to make a pickup for Ramos. You don't give the bags to anyone else, got it?" Jorge commanded.

"Yeah," Aaron said, nodding for emphasis. He went to the safe, opening it and taking out the bags that he'd put in there the night before. Jorge and Palmer took them and put them into backpacks before they both left.

Aaron was glad to see them go, and as soon as they were out the door, he signaled Denis that they were on the move. He heard the door to the other room open, then close about two minutes later. He'd been champing at the bit to see what was happening in there but knew that he had to bide his time because Diana looked like she wasn't messing around with her operation. Aaron counted footsteps for about forty-five seconds and guessed there were under ten people walking down the stairs. But definitely more than one. As soon as it was quiet, he went into the hall and picked the lock on the room.

It should be empty, but he wasn't taking any chances, so when he carefully turned the handle, he had his weapon in his right hand as he opened the door quickly and scanned the room. It was vacant and dirty. There was a bucket that had been used as a toilet. It smelled of sweat, blood and urine.

Making him gag. That potent cocktail of rage and revulsion went through him. This wasn't court-admissible evidence, but Aaron saw all he needed in order to know what this room was being used for. It sickened him and made him determined to put an end to the human trafficking going through this club.

Aaron double-checked the hallway before quickly documenting the room with the camera on his phone and then making sure to lock the door as he left. He tucked his weapon in the small of his back as he heard someone coming back up the stairs. He moved to his office doorway, which he'd left opened, and stepped out as a man he didn't recognize come into view.

"Who the hell are you?" the guy barked, pulling a SIG Sauer from his pocket.

"Quinn. Ramos brought me in to run this place," Aaron said smoothly. "And you?"

"Javier. I work for Diana. You stay out of the hallway until I knock on your door from now on. Got it?"

Quinn nodded. "No one mentioned that."

"I just did," Javier snapped. "Ramos knows better than to mess with Diana."

So the redhead was higher up than Ramos in the organization. Aaron just shrugged. "Fine by me."

He wasn't sure if he could get any more information from Javier, but figured it was worth a try. "So Ramos works for her?"

"He works for Perses."

A shot of adrenaline pumped through his veins. *Perses.* The shadowy head of the crime syndicate they were trying to bring down. He hadn't realized how close he'd been to the top when he got moved here to Mistral's.

But it made sense. Syndicates with lots of employees were harder to control. But this way you had a few top lieutenants and one big, shadowy boss man.

"Cool," Aaron said, going back into his office and closing the door. He wasn't sure what Javier was returning to the room for, but he hoped to find out soon. Meanwhile, Rick was meant to follow the van, and he texted Denis and Rick to see where each of the men were.

Heading west. Best guess Port of Los Angeles.

Aaron told Rick to keep him posted. Then his phone pinged with a message from Denis indicating that his guy was going toward the coast but more toward Malibu. So both men were moving.

Aaron knew he was done for the morning at Mistral's and left. He thought of going to his office, but he wanted to see what Steve had been up to and he also wanted to check with Lee. She was part of his current mission, but he knew that didn't justify him heading to Price Tower.

He ditched the van he drove as Quinn for a nondescript rental at his apartment, in case Ramos was having him followed, and then headed downtown to his office. He needed to update his boss on the room in the club and figure out how they were going to work that into the current operation.

Lee felt more rested when she woke up at eleven. She showered and packed a small bag to take to the apartment Aaron was using for his cover. Her old boss from the FBI had been in touch and Lee knew it was time to bring Van up to speed. She'd used the app to check in on Aaron's location. His warning for her to stay safe lingered in her mind. His role was much more dangerous and she wished she'd felt confident enough to ask the same of him.

She messaged Brody Hammond back and he told her to come into the field office for an update. Then she went to find Van. He was in his office, which was on the same floor as hers, and she saw him sitting behind his desk reading something on his computer when she walked in.

"Morning," he said.

"Morning. Thanks for sending Rick."

"No problem." He shot her a look. "Hammond just messaged me."

"I'm here to explain," Lee said.

He gestured to the guest chair in front of his desk. Sitting down in it, she wondered where to begin.

"So?"

She started talking, catching him up on everything that had happened the day before, from inadvertently getting pulled into Aaron's op to discovering the room at the top of the stairs. "I reached out to Hammond because I have the feeling we're dealing with human trafficking. And you know he's in charge of the task force."

"I do. Are you going to liaise with him on this?" Van asked.

"I'm not sure. He wants me to stop by the field office and have a debrief. I'm not sure if Isabell Montez fell into this or if she's separate from it," Lee said.

"What *do* you know?"

"She was at the club. My eyes told me it was the same place but the computer verified it," Lee told him. "I was going to take this to the cops, but with that locked room and the other signs pointing to some kind of trafficking, I think that Hammond would be better hands for it."

Van leaned back in his chair, crossing his massive arms over his chest. "I agree. And as much as I don't want you to get sucked back into that life, it seems like you are already."

"Yeah." She hesitated. "But that's not all…"

He raised an eyebrow at her. She took a deep breath. She'd pretty much decided she wasn't going to mention Cate to him. But sitting in his office across from him now, she knew she *had* to. There was no justification to keep quiet about it. *If* she was still alive and in LA, then Van needed to know.

"I saw someone last night who looked like Cate."

The air seemed to leave the room, and though Van didn't change position, she could tell he had tensed his body. He lifted one hand and rubbed it over his bald head before he leaned forward.

"*Looked* like or was?"

Lee shrugged and shook her head. "I can't confirm it, but I did get a good look at her…" She swallowed hard. "And a locked room, a missing girl and a woman who is her doppelgänger. I didn't want to wait to tell you. Plus, as we speak, Rick is trailing the van that definitely has young people in it."

"Okay, well, let's deal in facts. Keep Cate between you and me for now. I'll come with you to see Hammond," Van said.

"I can handle this," Lee protested.

"I know you can, but if it is Cate, then the fact that a girl was taken that your friend knew links this to us.

After Hammond, I want you to go talk to Boyd again and find out more about the girl's family connections."

"This is *my* case," she said.

"Sorry. Didn't mean to overstep." Van stared at her, and despite what he said, she knew deep down he wanted to take over. Had sort of guessed he would from the moment Cate's name came up. But that didn't mean she was going to just sit back and let him. "I was already planning to go and see Boyd again. I will continue to do that."

"I trust that you will. And, yeah, it *is* your op, Lee. But I want in. I'm not letting you face alone whatever she's bringing to us."

"I'm not positive—"

"You are or you wouldn't have come in here to talk to me or reached out to Hammond," Van said calmly. He wasn't asking her to confirm; he knew her that well.

"Yeah, I am. I mean, I have no proof, just my gut and that brief glimpse. I could be wrong."

"You usually aren't," Van said. "I'll drive to Hammond. Have Rick report to us there."

She nodded. "We're also looped in with the DEA."

"Okay, I assume Hammond's not going to object to sharing intel?" Van murmured.

"Too bad if he does. We're independent now and this case isn't his."

Her friend just gave her that slow smile of his that brimmed with pride. "That's right."

Lee knew that Van's first instinct was to protect his family, and that meant her, Rick and Aaron, because Aaron was Xander's brother. But he also knew that his family was strong and needed to stand on their own and handle this.

She wasn't sure what Hammond was going to say or what he'd tell them to do. But unless she actually was ordered to stop trying to find Isabell Montez, she was going to find the girl and hopefully take down Cate O'Dell in the process.

Chapter 10

The meeting with Aaron's boss made a few things clearer. The FBI Human Trafficking Task Force wanted to send in their own people, which Jayne had pushed back on. Jayne reminded him of Lee in a way. They were both ultra-efficient, smart and used to taking care of themselves. Too many new people were going to disrupt the operation and could jeopardize all the work they'd done to get Aaron in place.

"The woman, Lee Oscar, used to be an agent for them and they are going to use her, I believe. We should know more later," Jayne told him. "Denis has checked in and the location for the drop is at a house in Bel Air. We've got agents who will be watching it starting later today. While there, he got a ping about Steve... Want to tell me about that?"

Aaron rubbed the back of his neck and nodded. "Yeah. Lee set up a tracking app to show us his location. I think I mentioned it in my report. Denis put a small tracker on his car, and now when he moves, we are getting hits off cell phone towers as he goes past them."

"Good. He's the one who was in rival gang territory?"

"That's him. Did Denis say if he was back in Boyle Heights?"

"No, he's still on the Old Mission Trail," his boss said. "We should know more when he gets back. Rick Stone checked in as well. The van he was following got off before the port and he's watching the house where the people were moved. I passed that info on to Hammond, who will be taking over that surveillance for us."

"And keeping us in the loop?"

"Definitely. If Lee declines to work with the FBI again, then we'll have to have you end that relationship and bring in someone from their team." Jayne sighed. "Not ideal, but that's where we are at the moment. Let's hope she agrees to working with the FBI. How did she get involved to begin with?"

"She's looking for a missing teenager. The trail took her to Mistral's." Aaron cleared his throat, contemplating how much to say. "We know each other through my brother, just one of those things."

"Once she clocked you, you made a play to keep her quiet."

His boss knew what it was like being undercover and how every element had to be managed, even the unexpected. Though it had been Lee's idea for them to pretend to be a couple so she could get inside the club, he wasn't going to tell that to his boss. He nodded at Jayne. Lee was part of the op now and his feelings on the matter weren't going to be an issue. Had he ever felt this way about a woman before? No, of course not. But was he going to fuck up his mission? Hell no.

Aaron was *still* in control of the op, and he knew that

he was going to have to step up his role in the organization quicker than planned once the FBI got involved.

"Ramos reports to Perses," he added. "So I'm going
to try to take someone else down in the gang and move
up to get closer. I want to do that as soon as I can. But
I need to get a feel for everyone in and out of the club.
Jorge is definitely tight with Ramos, but there might be
a chink I can use to pry them apart. There are two lower-
level punks that I could also use if needed."

"Sounds like you have everything under control."

"Or as close to it as I can," Aaron said with a laugh.
"You know how it is undercover."

"Yes, I do. Every day is a new problem to solve. I
guess that's why you like it and I miss it."

Aaron rubbed the back of his neck again, feeling the
tension that had settled there as soon as Lee had become
involved. Another variable in this entire thing that was
adding to his uncertainty. Everything he'd thought he
knew about Lee had changed. He'd barely scraped the
surface of who she really was.

"Oh, hey, as a heads-up, there is a little complication,"
he said.

Jayne's face went completely blank, a frown furrow-
ing her brow. "Bad?"

Taking a deep breath, he crossed his arms over his
chest and tried to give off a nonchalant and totally not-
worried vibe. "Lee thought she recognized a woman last
night who was part of La Fortunata crime syndicate.
Cate O'Dell. She's known to the FBI, and Lee mentioned
that everyone believed O'Dell to be dead."

Turning back to her computer, Jayne's fingers started
moving over her keyboard and she leaned back, motion-

ing for Aaron to come around the back of her desk. The woman on the screen did resemble Diana. But it was hard to tell from the somewhat grainy, long-distance photo if they were the same person.

"That her?"

"Maybe. I could talk to a sketch artist or we can try to install some cameras, but there are people in and out of the club all the time," Aaron said.

"I'll get a second team on surveillance to watch for her. Do you think she'll come back again or was she there to meet you last night?"

"I think it was to meet me and approve me. Ramos is not her boss, and he said they were in charge of different operations, but he seemed wary of her," he replied.

"Interesting. She might be the big fish who can lead us to Perses."

"Exactly. I'll keep my eye for her and try to get closer to her if she shows up again. The guy who works for Perses is tough, but I could take him. I could start something with him and try to get in with her," Aaron suggested.

"We'll see." Jayne rubbed her chin, contemplating. "But first, we need to find out what Lee Oscar is going to do before we move this forward."

A part of Aaron hoped she turned the FBI down and walked away from him and this situation. He wanted her safe, but then part of what drew him to her was the fact that she wouldn't stop until there was justice. But he was pretty sure she wouldn't. Or, at least, the woman he thought he was starting to know wouldn't.

The FBI field office was in one of those government buildings that had been built in the '70s and really didn't stand out. Lee had wanted to take her Dodge but re-membered what Aaron had said about it being a flashy car. So she'd used a Toyota Prius that they kept in the garage. She missed the power of the Charger, but until she knew how big this missing-girl case had gotten, she wasn't taking any chances.

Van was with her since he insisted on coming along. He was in the passenger seat because he hated driving the Toyota. He'd been quiet on the way over, but that wasn't too unusual. Still, a part of her wondered if he was still processing the fact that Cate might be alive.

They were taken to a small meeting room and Ham-mond joined them a few minutes later.

"Price, didn't think I'd see you," Hammond said as he entered and held his hand out to Van first, and then to her, to shake.

"Thanks for coming down here, Oscar."

Hammond was in his fifties and fit. He looked like he'd been born in LA. His hair was thick and perfectly styled; his teeth were probably caps they were so white and straight, and his clothing was always fashionable and trendy. Lee knew that was just the image he wanted to project. He'd grown up back East and worked his way up the ranks in DC.

"Wasn't sure I had much choice," she said as they all sat down.

"There's always another option. But in this case it will be easier for all involved if you agree to work with us temporarily."

What? That wasn't what she'd been expecting. Van seemed to go still next to her as well. "I'll continue to work for Price but liaise with you and your team."

"That might work," Hammond said. "Right now, the DEA agent in charge, Jayne Montrose, doesn't want anyone new to interfere with her op. She said you are already known to the operative and to the gang they are infiltrating."

Hammond's statement was leading and Lee wasn't sure that he knew about her involvement and how much she could say without giving away Aaron's cover. "I…"

"Let me make this easier. We know about Quentin and his partner and that you are pretending to be his girlfriend to find…" He glanced down at the notes he had in front of him. "Isabell Montez."

Good that he already had that intel. "The cops aren't putting much effort into finding her and it looks like she might have run away, but I didn't want to leave any loose ends. There is a photo of the girl at Mistral's, which I confirmed last night. Now with the human trafficking, I'm not sure that she ran off. Her last known address was broken into and ransacked. Not sure if that ties with this in any way."

"We don't know either," Hammond said. "What is the address? I'll have our people look into it and see if there is any connection to this operation you stumbled into."

"I think Agent Quentin was surprised by the holding room for people in the club. Though it's noisy at night and no one is there during the day, so it is sort of ideal for a stash house."

"It is. We were working another location on the Old Mission Trail. I believe Rick Stone—he works for you, Price, right?—is there now."

"He does work for us. He checked in from a location

where the people were moved to," Van confirmed. "Was it known to you?"

"We suspected it might be a location they were using. We think this is a branch of La Fortunata. They operate the way they used to," Hammond said.

Lee glanced over at Van. He gave her a small nod.

"I thought I saw Cate O'Dell last night. I only got a glimpse of her. I believe she's using the name Diana and is somehow connected to the gang that Aaron is investigating," Lee said.

"O'Dell was reported deceased," Hammond said. "Are you sure?"

"I'm not unsure." Because that was the truth at this moment. She couldn't rule that woman out as Cate and until she did no one was going to be safe. Cate was ruthless and would do anything to please her father, who they suspected was the shadowy head of La Fortunata known only as Perses.

"Then, I'm going to have to do the hard sell to keep you on this operation, Oscar. You know Cate better than anyone but Price. If she's involved, then we know we are close to the top of the organization and we could take it down for good."

If only it would be as easy as he was making it sound. "I'll report to you each day and keep you in the loop, but I'm not working for you."

Hammond looked like he was going to put up a fight, but Van leaned forward. "You owe us. You used her and me without any compunction, setting us up with O'Dell to see how far her deception would go and how far she'd take us. Lee will work with you but not *for* you, and when this is over you don't contact us again," Van said.

Hammond leaned back in his chair, swiveling it from side to side. "I'll have to check with my boss. I'll see what I can do."

He got up and left the room. She turned to Van. "Thanks for having my back."

"You know I always do."

Aaron wasn't surprised that Lee had agreed to continue working with him on this operation. He was relieved not to have to try to bring someone else in, because that would have been difficult, but he would have managed it. Also he just wanted to keep working with Lee.

The attraction between them lent a believability to the charade of them being lovers, which would be harder to get Ramos to buy with a new woman at this point, because he really wanted Lee. There was a tension between them that he knew couldn't really be faked.

"The FBI briefed her on what they have and you know everything we have. Meet with her back at the apartment. In fact, after today I want you to be full time on the gang. It feels like everything is going to break sooner than we expected. Denis will be a regular at the club and you can pass info to him via Lee," Jayne said. "Push to get close to Ramos and his boss. We need to get the proof of the connection to Perses."

"Got it. I'll send reports each day. I think that with the hours at the club, the reports are going to be short," Aaron said.

"That works," Jayne said.

Aaron left a few minutes later and realized that, once he walked out of the building, he wasn't going to be

Aaron Quentin for a while. It was time to shed that man and to wholly become Quinn. He left his car at the office and took the bus back to his apartment. As usual, his attention was on high alert, watching the passengers around him from behind his sunglasses. He didn't think he'd been followed earlier or now. But he wasn't taking any chances. He had to walk three blocks from where he got off the bus to his apartment in Echo Lake, and when he got there, he spotted Lee sitting outside the apartment with her back against the door. His breath caught in his chest as it always did when he saw her.

This was getting…out of hand. He'd never been a man ruled by lust, but with her… She was always in his mind. Right now, that was a danger to both of them.

She had her laptop open and her fingers were moving over the keyboard. She looked up when she heard him on the stairs. She closed the computer and stood up.

"Hey. Forgot to get a key from you," she said.

"Yeah, we'll fix that today," he murmured, noticing she had a duffel bag and a large computer bag with her. He knew she was here to stay for the duration of the operation as well.

As soon as they were inside, he leaned against the door, watching her stand sort of awkwardly in the middle of the living/dining room area.

"You're working with the FBI now?"

"Sort of. Still working for Price, just reporting to my old boss. They wanted me back on staff, but that was a no-go. Your boss okay with this?" she asked.

"She kind of had no choice. But yeah. I'm glad you said yes."

"I wasn't going to say no. I still don't know what happened to Isabell, and there is a chance that she's been moved through the club. I want to find her and put a stop to the human trafficking operation."

"Do you have any idea why they are taking teens from this area?"

"The FBI doesn't know, but then they didn't know about the connection to your drug gang. My theory is that it might be to pay debts. Could that be a thing? I mean the way the Montez house was turned over, it was clear they were looking for something," Lee said.

Aaron walked farther into the room as she put her computer bag on the floor next to the table and set down her laptop. "That house was in Boyle Heights?"

"Yes. Which reminds me I need to follow up on the fingerprints from Detective Monroe."

"We were at a house in the same neighborhood, making a bust that same day. It's interesting because there is a rival gang who operates there, but they had infiltrated the Cachorros and I was able to use that to move up the ranks."

"That is interesting… Use that information how?"

"I burned the other gang member," Aaron said.

"Burned?"

"Ratted him out so I could gain trust," he explained.

"What happened to him?" Lee asked.

Aaron wasn't sure how much Lee understood of working undercover in criminal gangs. "They made an example of him and dropped his body back at his old gang's hangout."

"Did you know they'd do that?"

"I did. We might need to do something violent at the club. You going to be okay with that?"

She didn't answer him, but he saw on her face that she wasn't going to be. "I'm trying to protect people, babe. Sometimes that means picking an innocent life over one that has been corrupting innocents. If you can't handle it, you should back out now. I'll look for your girl."

Lee pursed her lips and shook her head. "No, I get it. I forgot about that side of being undercover. We're mainly a bodyguard service… We protect, and though sometimes that means firing a shot, I'm in the office watching over everyone. It's just been a long time for me."

"It's okay. This life, it's not for everyone. No one is going to think less of you if you say no and go back to Price Tower," he said. He would be disappointed because he wanted to spend more time with her, and not just because of the job, but he didn't want her to have to do anything that made her uncomfortable.

"I would think less of *myself*. Isabell might have been traded for her parents' debts, and I can't just walk away from that or from people who would take a child that way."

He got it. "Good. I'll try to keep you away from that."

"You don't have to," she said. "You don't have to protect me."

"But I want to," he ground out. Even though he knew he should have kept that sentiment to himself. It was the truth and she deserved that and so much more from him.

Chapter 11

Protect her. It wasn't a sentiment that she'd ever heard from anyone else. Maybe her grandpa had made her feel safe... No *maybe* about it, the old man had kept her safe. But he'd been the only one. She'd learned to fend for herself at a young age and had never forgotten those lessons.

"Thanks. But I got me," she said, sitting down at the table. Aaron dropped into the chair next to her.

"I know. I've seen you rolling with whatever is thrown your way," he told her gruffly. "I'm the same."

"Oh, I know that, but you do it in a different way. I'm in a corner trying to get as much information as I can to figure out how to get the upper hand, while you're in the center of it dancing around and changing to suit the environment. Why do you do that?" she asked.

He rubbed the back of his neck. The question was personal. *Too personal?* Maybe, but she wanted to know. There was no denying that part of the reason she was here with Aaron was the man himself. In fact, she wouldn't have gotten this close to Cate or working with her old task force again without him.

She also wouldn't be closer to piecing together a theory on what happened to Isabell Montez. It wasn't lost on Lee that the more days that passed, the less likely it was that they were going to get that girl back alive. She needed to be here to save her. And knew that her hero complex was as strong as Aaron's.

But she was also here *for* him.

She wanted him, and the time apart hadn't lessened those feelings. At this moment, everything felt out of control, including herself, and the one solid in the maelstrom was Aaron.

"I don't know," he said with a shrug and then turned back to facing the table, his hands steepled together.

"I thought you said there would be no lies when we were undercover. That lying increased our chances of failure."

He let out a long, hard breath. "Do you want to do this? I'm not a man for half measures, Lee. If I start opening up to you, then I'm going to have you in my bed and we both said that wasn't a good idea."

"Don't I get a say?" she asked.

"Of course you do. But we both know you won't say no," he muttered. Then crossed his arms over his chest as he used his feet to turn the chair he was sitting on toward her. "Would you?"

She chewed her lower lip. *No lies.* She should have guessed that he would push back. Aaron was a predator. He was always going to go after any weakness, but that was tempered with that need to protect. She wanted to know what had made this complex man the way he was.

His brother Xander also had this solid core of protectiveness and remoteness. What happened in their upbringing to shape them this way?

"Do you know much about the Quentins?" he asked.

She shrugged, flashing him a coy look. "Some. I mean, I know you're all big, British, stubborn and trustworthy."

"Thanks for that. *Stubborn* though? Isn't that a bit of projecting?" he asked, his mouth lifting on one side in a slight smile.

"Perhaps. So…"

"We are all close in age—all four of us—and we grew up like a pack. Fighting each other to be the dominant, protecting each other from anyone outside who threatened. It was a rough-and-tumble childhood where my mom did her best but we were a lot."

"Sounds interesting," she murmured, unable to fathom the kind of childhood he was describing. She'd always been alone. Even at Grandpa's bar, she'd been by herself in the back, staying out of sight. She'd always known how to be quiet and keep out of the way.

"Probably sounds nuts to you, but the truth is we are all alphas, so we fight everyone and everywhere. It made my life difficult until…"

He trailed off and shook his head. "I had to leave the family and it was a wake-up call. I couldn't be the alpha out in the world without getting into a lot of scuffles and ending up in jail. So I took a few classes at a community college in Florida and started to get into law enforcement. It gave me some discipline that I didn't realize I had been lacking. The rest is history, as you Yanks say."

A glossed-over version of who he was, but it gave her some insight into him. "Every time you say 'Yank,' it reminds me of some Southern folks who'd strongly state they are *not* a Yankee."

"Yeah, there were a few folks in Florida who didn't

appreciate being called that," he chuckled. "What about you? Why are you in the corner gathering intel?"

Hmm. What to tell him? Her past was so typical, she thought. So many kids grew up in a bad family situation, and while that didn't make it right, she'd never wanted that to be what defined her. "Dad with a temper, mom with a drinking problem. I learned if I was quiet and stayed out of the way, things went better for me. So I was sort of training for my job in childhood." She glanced over at him. "I guess you were too. Learning to fight and protect your pack. But undercover, you're alone. How does that feel?" she asked. Feeling pretty proud of herself that she'd answered his question and then turned the spotlight back on him.

Because the last thing she wanted to do was to talk about her past or her childhood. That one bit she'd shared was enough. Gave him a picture and he could draw in the rest, because she wasn't one for rehashing.

"Nice try, babe."

She furrowed her brow. "Huh?"

"I see what you're doing. And it's not going to work. I told you I'm used to being the alpha, and I do that with my strength. And you are used to being the alpha too, but you do it with your mind. And there was a time when you'd get me talking about myself without returning the favor. But you haven't really told me anything yet."

"I doubt there was ever a time when you talked about yourself. You play it close to the vest," she said.

"Just like you."

She'd opened up the past and now he wanted to know more about her. Trusting her with his back wasn't as difficult as it would be with a stranger. Her relationship with Xander made her sort of a known quantity. Plus she'd stood by his brother more than once.

That was great and all, but he needed to know what made her tick. What were her weaknesses and when was she going to crumble? Everyone crumbled at some point, and it was important to know what would trigger her. He knew his own triggers and Denis's—both of them had worked together for long enough to realize when the other one needed a break before they shattered.

But Lee wasn't like him or anyone else he'd worked with before. How she'd handle everything in the club and the investigation, he wasn't sure. Last night she'd been solid, but he saw her try to push her way in when he'd been with Ramos. She'd backed down, but there might come a time when she wouldn't.

She was looking for a missing teen and he had to wonder why. This clearly wasn't a Price Security gig, and she'd given little away on that front. "Why are you looking for this girl?"

"A friend asked—"

"I'm going to stop you there. You already told me that, but I want to know *why you*? Why did the friend come to you? You work for a bodyguard firm."

She sort of went white and looked down at her laptop screen. It was open, but the screen was black and had gone to sleep while they were talking. He saw her fingers flex and he knew she wanted to start typing on the keyboard and disappear into the web of information that she was weaving. But he wasn't going to let her.

This could be her crucial weakness and he needed to know it.

"Uh… Boyd and I went to high school together. My best friend was his girlfriend, and she disappeared one day after school. It's definitely the reason I wanted to join the FBI and get on the human trafficking task force. After I retired, Boyd still gets in touch when he notices things with his students. He's a high school chemistry teacher."

There was more here beneath the surface than he was picking up on. He knew that and pushed it into the back of his mind to analyze later. "Are you trying to save the friend you couldn't?"

"Are you trying to save the brother you injured?" she countered.

That froze him in his tracks. He wasn't aware she knew about Tony and what had happened. Aaron's rough rugby tackle on an uneven field in the mud. Tony's head had hit the ground hard, and a rock that no one had noticed damaged his spinal cord, leaving his brother paralyzed from the waist down.

She'd done it again. Turned things back on him to keep from revealing too much. There was a time when Aaron would have walked away, but he and Xander had been talking and he'd talked to Tony as well. Things were getting better there. "I'm not hamstrung by my past anymore. But you still are."

She shrugged and looked away. "I'm not sure what any of this matters. You don't need to know about my childhood."

"Actually, I do. You are part of my team now. I can't keep you safe if I don't know what is going to break you."

"Nothing's going to 'break' me. I'm strong and can

take way more than anything this crime syndicate is going to dish out," she said.

"I don't know that. I've never seen you under pressure and past the point of exhaustion. Living two lives and moving an investigation forward inch by impossibly slow inch. So I'm going to prod and probe until I know all of your secrets."

She chewed her lip again and then shook her head. "I can't talk about it. It's all tied up in guilt and drive and ambition. I'm a loner because that's easier for me."

"You're not a loner at Price. You're a big part of that team," Aaron pointed out, tucking that other fact away.

"I'm in the tower. I'm watching and directing them. I make them keep in touch at all times. I don't let anyone out of my sight. That's my weakness. When I can't find someone I sort of get frantic. I have to know where the people I care about are."

"So you don't lose them. This girl… You want to find her for your friend so he doesn't lose someone else."

She was a protector, like him. The incident that shaped her happened about the same age as his had. That type of thing had a way of leaving a mark on the soul. One that wasn't going to go away.

"So you go frantic, how?" he asked.

"I get information. Find the weakness in someone else and I attack. I do whatever I can to get them back. And while I don't know Isabell, Boyd did, and he thinks she's worth saving, so I'm going to gather every bit of information I can find and I'm going to find her."

Or her body, but he didn't say that out loud.

"Okay. I learned that it took more than strength to be strong after Tony's accident. It was a tough lesson to learn and took me years to recognize, but that's where I am." A muscle ticked in his jaw. "My temper is my weakness. If I get pushed too hard and too long, I snap and then I'm a danger to everyone." He turned toward her, pinning his gaze on hers. "Denis's weakness is a bit like yours. He has to know where all the players are. He'll put himself in danger to find me if I miss a check-in. He'll do the same for you, so never miss one."

"I won't," she said. "Am I part of the team now?"

He nodded.

Aaron was still tense from that moment she'd asked about his brother Tony, which had been a dick move. But when she felt attacked, she always came out swing-ing. No matter that she understood what he was doing.

She should apologize but wasn't really sure how to go about it. "So who is on your team?"

A distraction from what she truly wanted to do, which was just go over to him, climb on his lap and put her arms around him. But a hug wasn't going to take away the sting of her words. Information had always seemed more dangerous than physical strength to Lee. It gave her a bonus hit point in the game of life against most people who were content to take the news at face value and bump along the path of their lives.

Not her. She'd always been digging deeper and pull-ing out little tidbits that she tucked away to use as ammo when she was backed into a corner.

"Denis and my boss, Jayne. Rick is also going to be part of it. Price agreed to let him work with us on this. He's got good instincts."

"Rick's the best. I wasn't seeing the drug connection

to Isabell's disappearance at first," Lee admitted. "If you give me their cell numbers, I can add them to a tracking app that I use so I can keep tabs on them."

"I will," he said, standing up and starting to move away from her.

"Where are you going?"

"We have some downtime before we have to get to the club, and I want to pinpoint the houses that Jayne mentioned to see if I can find a pattern."

"I can help with that," she offered.

"I'm sure you can, but I need some alone time."

He left the main living area of the apartment, and a few minutes later, she heard the shower come on in the bathroom. It was hard to wait for him to be done. The guilt she felt over hitting him with that accident wouldn't let her just sit still. She waited a good ten minutes—surely that was enough time for him to get dressed—before she got up and went to the bedroom.

She knocked on the door.

"Yes."

He didn't open it or invite her to enter. Leaning her head against the wood door, she closed her eyes.

"I'm sorry."

He didn't say anything. She knew he had to have heard her, and a moment later, the door opened, almost catching her off guard. He stood there, wearing a towel wrapped around his hips. His big, muscled torso was bare and she wasn't going to lie. She couldn't take her eyes off him.

He had those big biceps that she found attractive and a long scar that ran from his left shoulder down toward his nipple. She shamelessly continued to drink in the sight of him. He had a light dusting of hair on his chest, which grew narrower as her gaze dropped down and saw where it disappeared into the towel.

He put one arm up on the doorjamb and stood there, letting her look at him. God, when was she going to stop making mistakes with this man?

Probably never.

Realizing she was still staring at his chest, she closed her eyes and took a deep breath.

"I shouldn't have brought your brother into things earlier. I was feeling pushed into a corner and just used the only ammunition I had that I thought would make you back down," she admitted. "I'm sorry."

She kept her eyes closed because if she opened them again and saw his bare chest and the bed right behind him, she might do something impulsive. No *might* about it, she thought. She was definitely going to—

His finger brushed over her cheek and then pushed a strand of hair behind her ear. "I'm sorry too."

"Sorry? For what?"

"For cornering you. You're too good at revealing nothing of yourself and I want to know more."

"For the mission," she whispered, still not opening her eyes because she was afraid if she did, he'd stop touching her.

"No," he said.

His forehead rested against hers and the softness of his exhalation brushed over her mouth, making her lips tingle. She did open her eyes then. Her heart beat faster, seeing him so close. Their eyes met and she realized she was holding her breath, waiting for…something. For him to make the next move?

The truth was, she wasn't certain what exactly she was waiting for, but she wasn't sure of herself with him. Which was so unlike her.

But she was *done* waiting.

She lifted her hand and cupped his jaw. He'd shaved, so the skin was so smooth she couldn't help running her finger over it. Then she tipped her head to the side, leaned up and kissed him.

A real first kiss. Not one for show but one that they both wanted. One that was just for the two of them. His lips were firm and he kissed her back. His mouth opening slowly as she sucked his bottom lip into her mouth. He tasted good and minty.

His hand stayed gently against the side of her neck and she kept her hand on his jaw. That was it. They were barely touching, but she felt flayed bare to her soul. The need for Aaron was so strong inside of her that she was on fire.

He lifted his head and their eyes met. Watching her, he was waiting to see what she would do next. She splayed her hand in the center of his chest and just stood there, her heart in her throat, conveying with her touch that she was all-in. The next thing she knew, his arm went around her waist and he lifted her off her feet, pulling her into that big, strong body of his. She wrapped her legs around his hips and her arms around his shoulders and kissed him again.

Knowing that this was the only place she wanted to be right now. The only place that felt right, and for the first time since her grandpa had died...the only place where she felt safe.

Chapter 12

All his life, he'd been strong and unbreakable. No one understood better than him what a fairy tale that belief had been. He'd thought of his brothers, the Quentin boys, as unbeatable as well. But one rough tackle had shown him the lie of that and he'd never been the same since.

Not once.

That Lee had known that was his weakness and had gone straight for it to even the playing field told him how much she hated being vulnerable. It was odd to look down into her face and admit to himself just how much alike they were. There was no comfort in it.

Her apology... That was the one thing he'd never been able to figure out how to do. Of course he knew he just had to say the words *I'm sorry*, but they never came. Not once.

Then she had kissed him, turned him on with her apology and her kiss. She had a rocking body that he had been noticing the last few times they met. Something about dealing with Xander and that entire situation meant the first time she'd just been one of the Price Security team and not a woman. Even when they'd been doing shots and flirting, it had been more of a blowing-off-steam thing in South Florida. Now…this was any-thing but. This was a need-to-have-Lee-in-his-arms thing. He hadn't noticed how thick her eyebrows were or how, up close, those brown eyes of hers actually had flecks of green and gold in them.

She had pretty eyes.

"Aaron?"

Just his name, but as a question. Why was he hesitat-ing? That had to be what she wanted to know. But she'd been up-front with him in the past. She hadn't wanted to have sex with him back in South Beach because she liked him.

"Do you still like me?" he gritted out. Because he *really* liked her. She was in the middle of an operation and part of his cover now, so that complicated things. *Ya think?*

But she was so close that he could smell that subtle floral fragrance that he only associated with her each time he took a breath. So close that the heat of her body was making him hotter and harder than he'd been in a long time. So close that complications were melting away and a more primal instinct was taking over.

"Yes," she murmured. "Do you?"

He turned and felt the towel he'd knotted around his hips slip. It fell to the floor as he shifted and walked with her to the bed. "What do you think?"

His hard-on was pressed against her and she had shifted as he was walking, tightening her legs around his hips. Her hands were in his hair and he knew that if he was going to stop, it would have to be now.

"Do you want this?" he rasped. "We're still under-cover, still living a lie."

"Yes."

Just one word but so damned confident and sure that his cock jumped, and he knew this wasn't going to be one of those take-him-a-while-to-get-going sessions. He had been wanting her for too long, yearning for her more and more since he'd seen her at the police station…

He set her on her feet, his hands going to the waistband of her jeans. He undid them, hearing the button pop in the quiet room, and then she brushed his hands aside, twisting her hips and pushing her jeans and underwear down her legs.

She still had her shoes on, so she had to lean down to toe them off. As she did so, he felt the warmth of her breath against his naked legs and couldn't help running his hands over her back and down to her butt as she bent toward him.

"You have a fine ass," he said.

Which made her laugh. "Thanks."

Lee stood up slowly and then put her hands on the hem of her shirt, but he stopped her. He wanted to undress her, not just watch her strip for him. He pulled the shirt up and over her head. Once it was off, he looked down at her body with her small belly and curvy hips. Her breasts were full, her skin sort of olive-toned. He reached behind her with one hand to undo her bra, but her hand found his cock, fisting him, and he forgot about everything but the pleasure of her touch.

God, that felt good. As she stroked him, he rocked his hips into her touch. She squeezed him as she went up his length, running her finger around the rim at the tip and then moving back down. He shook when he felt her mouth on the base of his neck, sucking his skin.

It took more concentration than he wanted to admit to get her bra undone before peeling it away from her breasts.

Aaron cupped her breasts in his palms, rubbing her tight reddish-brown nipples with his thumbs. She arched her back and returned the favor by stroking him faster. He was close to coming and hadn't felt like this since he'd been in his twenties. He took her hand from him and gently pushed her until she fell back on the bed.

Her hair spread out around her head, her legs fell open and his breath caught in his chest. He'd had sex fairly regularly over the last few years, but it had been a lifetime since he'd made love to a woman that he liked and cared about.

He didn't want to rush this. He didn't want to ruin this by coming too fast or not being what she needed. But he *did* know that once he and Lee hooked up, nothing was going to be the same again. He put his knee on the bed and leaned over her. Wanted to take his time with her but also to take her as fast as he could so that she would finally be his.

Well, be his for as long as he could hold her. If there was one thing that Aaron Quentin knew, it was that nothing lasted forever and that he needed to savor every moment, which was exactly what he intended to do with Lee.

There was no use in pretending that she wasn't going to keep falling for Aaron while they worked together. So why deny herself this? Lee had no idea what the world would be like for them when they finished this operation, but she knew that she'd regret it if she didn't give everything of herself to him while they were together.

Coming to apologize had been hard. Admitting she wasn't her best self always was, but she'd known she had to acknowledge her shortcomings and was glad she had. Aaron reminded her so much of how she could have been if not for Van and the team at Price Security. A loner. But now that he was slowly moving up her body, she couldn't really think about anything except the aching emptiness between her legs and how much she needed him inside of her.

He had lean hips but strong, muscled legs. Everything about this man was better than she'd expected. He had lifted her easily into his arms, and that was no small feat given she was a big girl. But he'd done it without much strain. There was something about that that had really touched her in a way she hadn't expected.

She reached between them as he sucked her nipple into his mouth and found his erection. His hips canted forward and she stroked him. Then couldn't help rubbing the tip of his cock against her clit. That felt so good as his mouth was sucking on her. Her hips writhed against him and she realized she was going to come if she kept touching herself with his dick.

His dick.

She let go of him. "Aaron."

He lifted his head, and her nipple tightened even more from the coolness in the room.

"Do you have a condom? I'm on the pill, but I don't like to take chances with pregnancy or STDs… I know, such sexy talk—"

He put his hand over her mouth, smiling down at her.

"It's sexy to know you care about yourself. I do. Give me a second."

He got off the bed and she watched the fluidity of his movements as he walked to the bathroom and returned a moment later, putting the condom on as he came back to her. Her heart beat faster at the sight of him. How natural he was in his own body and with her. She appreciated that.

"Where was I?" he asked as he knelt between her legs again.

She pointed to her breast but then opened her arms and legs. "But I don't need more teasing. I want you inside of me."

A guttural sound came from him as he fell on her. His mouth found hers and his hips shifted until she felt the tip of him at the entrance of her body. She opened her thighs wider and lifted her hips as she wrapped her legs around him. His tongue pushed deep into her mouth, rubbing over hers, and she sucked on his in return. Then, lifting her hips, she found herself pushing down with her heels on the small of his back, but still he didn't enter her.

His mouth just moved on hers, his tongue plunging deeper. And as she arched her back, he shifted his chest against her, the hair on his chest rubbing against her already hardened nipples, making her moan deep in her throat and try harder to get him inside of her.

One hand moved down the side of her body and she felt his finger on her clit, rubbing and tapping against it. He lifted his head and growled, "Come for me and I'll take you."

It wasn't that hard to come. His chest against her

breasts, his hand on her center…that teasing tip of his dick inside of her. She pulled his head back to hers and sucked hard on his tongue, arching her hips against each movement of his hand until she felt everything in her body tightening and cresting as stars danced between her eyes and she came hard.

He didn't need her to tell him; he just made that deep groan again and thrust all the way inside of her. He held himself there, deep in her, as her body continued spasming, now around his cock. She opened her eyes and saw he was watching her. He put his forehead against hers as he started to drive into her again and again. Going deeper and deeper every time, until she felt her orgasm building again. She used her heels on his back to urge him to keep going, and he did until she cried out his name.

He pushed one hand under their bodies and grabbed her butt, lifting her up into his thrusts and driving harder and faster and deeper. Until she heard him bellow out too, and felt his cock got bigger inside of her, but he kept on thrusting. Until he came.

She wrapped her arms around him as he rested his head against her shoulder. Lee kept her legs around his hips, holding him to her, as her hand tenderly moved over his back as he came back to himself. This man that she was realistic enough to know she wasn't going to hold forever was hers. He was hers *for now* and that was all that mattered.

She knew that she would do whatever she had to in order to keep him safe. That her circle of family had grown larger, and she didn't allow herself to sit in the thought, but she knew that Aaron was more than family. More than a lover or even a potential boyfriend. He was the man that she could care more deeply about than anyone else.

And that frightened her. She hadn't let anything frighten her this much since Hannah had disappeared.

Aaron didn't want to move. But he also didn't want to acknowledge the emotions that she stirred in him. Life was easier when he was focused on the job and not on people or his connection to them.

He knew it was fucked-up that he didn't know how to emote except physically. Lee wouldn't know that this was him pretty much telling her how he felt. But he did. And it shook him.

She was stroking his back and he shifted his weight so that he rested on his hip, off her, and let her touch him. There had been so few gentle touches like this in his life. Maybe his mom before he'd tackled Tony, but after that, Aaron hadn't felt worthy of being comforted. He wasn't sure he still was, but for right now none of that mattered. He just lay in her arms, breathing in that floral scent that was hers and taking comfort from that warm, feminine body beneath his.

Except it wasn't just a feminine body. It was Lee. He was very aware of who he was here with and how much he wanted to keep her in his arms for longer than they had. But he knew his alarm was going to go off in a few minutes, and he had to go on a call with his boss to update her on his progress.

"I can feel you shifting into work mode," she murmured.

He lifted his head, their eyes met and he wished…

Well, not that he was a different man because as messed up as he was inside, he didn't want to be anyone else but Aaron Quentin. But he wished they'd met at another time, under different circumstances. However, when was he going to meet a woman like Lee Oscar *except* when he was undercover?

All either of them did was work.

That was a truth he would do well not to forget.

"Yeah. Sorry about that."

"No, it's cool. I'll get a shower and then I can help you with linking the houses," she said, then chewed her lower lip between her teeth. "Are we good now?"

He had to smile at the way she'd asked it. "We're better than good. Sorry I got my—"

She put her long, cool fingers against his mouth. "You don't owe me an apology."

"Well, you're getting it," he muttered, shifting on top of her again and rolling until their positions were reversed. She put her arms on his chest and lifted her head up to look down on him.

The long curtain of her hair fell around them, brushing his chest and tickling against his neck, and he closed his eyes as he felt himself stir. Getting turned on by her. But at thirty-eight, he knew the chances of him going again were, well, not realistic. But he wanted to.

"Thanks, then," she said.

His alarm started going off before he could say anything else. Sitting up, he shifted her to the bed next to him, then went to the dresser where he'd left his phone and turned off the alarm. "I've got a call in five."

She got up too and came over, wrapping her arms around him from the back and hugging him. She kissed the middle of his back and then walked into the bathroom. He followed her because he had to deal with the condom and wash up and finish getting ready.

She acted so natural as she grabbed a towel and got in the shower. Going over to the sink to brush his teeth and wash up, he realized he was surprised by that. But then knew he shouldn't be. Lee wasn't going to do a whole postmortem on having sex with him during an undercover operation. She didn't need to. They'd both said everything that needed to be said earlier.

Now they were in uncharted territory; whatever happened next would be new. To them both. He wanted to believe that in some way this would be okay, but that was never the case when he was undercover. Hell, the last time, he'd been working in a coffee shop and ended up putting his boss, Obie Keller, in danger in the swamp. It had only been the fact that he'd reached out to his brother that had saved her.

This time Aaron knew he was going to have to protect Lee. She was the kind of woman who would take risks and put herself in danger to make sure the operation was a success. He understood how important it was to her to find the missing girl and catch the people responsible for taking her, if that was the case. He exhaled roughly, shoving a comb through his hair. There was still so much work to do and his concentration should be focused on that.

Not on Lee showering behind him. Or the fact that he wanted to take her back to bed, pretend that this apartment was anywhere but in Los Angeles. He wanted a life with her. He'd never let himself need anyone. Never. So these emotions swirling around inside him scared him more than anything he'd ever faced undercover.

And that made him hurry through washing up and getting away from her.

But there was no life with Lee or anyone else. Not for him. He wasn't being dramatic. That was the truth. He kept his balance by living undercover. By protecting people who would never know what he did.

He'd tried getting close to someone once, ten years ago, and it had been a disaster.

His life had crashed and burned, and he hadn't allowed himself to get personal since then.

He went into the bedroom to get dressed, thinking that he wanted to believe he'd changed since then, but the truth was there hadn't been anyone he'd allowed himself to care for in that decade. He hadn't even gone home or talked to his brothers.

Not until he had reached out to Xander, and nothing had been the same since then.

Nothing.

Chapter 13

When Lee got out of the shower, she noticed that Aaron had brought her duffel bag into the bedroom and left it on the bed. She left her hair to dry naturally and put on a pair of faded jeans and a short-sleeved T-shirt.

Strangely she wasn't overanalyzing what had happened with Aaron. She knew at some point it was going to hit her, but for now, it seemed like she was cool with it. Or as chill as she *could* be, starting an affair while working undercover for the FBI again. But it was harder than she'd thought it would be.

That woman she'd been back when she was employed by the FBI was so different from the one she was now. Sometimes it felt like she hadn't changed a bit, but this afternoon had shown her just how much she had.

Even so, she had to be careful that she didn't let this thing with Aaron get in the way of the job. The more days that went by without finding Isabell Montez, the more worried she was for the girl.

Heading into the living room, she saw Aaron was on a video call with his boss, Jayne, and his partner, Denis. She also recognized a familiar figure in the background, fellow Price Security employee Rick Stone.

Aaron turned when she walked out and gave her a half smile. "We need your help tracking some addresses. Rick and Denis each went to different locations, but Rick said you noticed they were on the Old Mission Trail or as it is also known the Camino Real."

Lee moved to her keyboard and felt a sense of calm come over her. Yeah, this was what she needed. Nothing got her back to her center like working on a problem on her computer. "Did you enter them in the database, Rick?"

"Yeah. It pinged a pattern, but you know me and technology. I tried to tap it, but then it got messed up. Can you look at it?" he asked.

"Of course," she said, accessing Rick's files remotely and pulling up the geotags he'd put in for the location he'd visited, plus the one Denis had. There was a third address in there as well. "What's the other place?"

"That's a known drop house where weighing and packaging takes place. Also we can add the house in Boyle Heights for money counting. Mistral's as a…" He trailed off, not entirely sure, but it seemed like everything was in close proximity to Mistral's. "Is it central?" Aaron asked, coming to lean over her as her fingers moved on the keyboard, putting in the coordinates for each of them. It wasn't exactly on the Old Mission Trail, but it was pretty close, and all of the locations circled around Boyle Heights.

"It seems like this is the area they are operating in," she said, pointing to her screen.

"Share it to the video call," Aaron told her.

Nodding, she connected wirelessly to his device and

shared her screen. While the others were looking at it, she added labels to each area.

"Could you add in where Steve has been traveling?" Denis asked. "I think that we might be seeing two gangs covering the same territory."

She pulled up the algorithm she'd written for him and Aaron to use and loaded those coordinates into the map. There was a small bit of overlap in Boyle Heights, but then Steve was handling things more toward the coast and San Clemente, also a stop on the Old Mission Trail.

"What's in this overlapping area?" Aaron asked. "It's hard to tell if Steve's working just for the Cachorros or if he's also a player for the Chacals."

"Or is he independent, reporting to someone else?" Rick murmured. "La Fortunata syndicate runs deep and has connections to almost everyone. Is there a chance Steve is more direct to them—not really part of either of the two gangs?"

"He was near the house where you saw the teens taken," Lee confirmed. Thinking that possibly that meant Steve was working for La Fortunata. "But why is he playing at being part of the other gangs if that's the case?"

"We don't have a name or photo for Perses," Denis reminded them.

Aaron looked over at her. "Do you have one of Steve?"

He and Denis both went to their devices, as did Rick, all three men trying to go through the surveillance footage they'd taken. "Send it all to me. I can collate and pull out individual faces."

"Great," Rick said, sending his first.

"How quick will it be?" Aaron asked.

"Not that fast, unfortunately," she replied. "It takes

time to run their faces through the databases I have access to so we can identify them. Then you can tell us what name you know these guys by," Lee said.

Denis kept studying the map. Then a moment later, the door opened and Lee noticed her former boss from the FBI and Aaron's boss enter the room. She guessed that their display was up on a big screen because both of them moved closer to it.

"This is where the teens are?" Hammond asked.

"That's where the van stopped and I saw them transferred inside. Not sure if they are still there. I left after the van did and followed it," Rick confirmed.

"Where did it go?" Hammond asked him.

"Toward the Port of Los Angeles," he said. "They turned into this residential area and it was harder to tail them, but my guess is to one of these houses."

Rick leaned forward to touch the screen. "I can't see where you are tapping," Lee told him. "Give me the map coordinates and I'll put a circle on the area."

He gave them to her and she indicated them.

Then she sat back to look at the track. They now had a pretty large circle that the gang was operating in. "We need to get into that house. I can't get a warrant without more than this. Any chance you can get into it, Aaron?"

He went still and Lee turned, watching as a calm came over him. It was almost as if she could hear the wheels turning in his mind.

"I'd have to start something and take down Jorge, but yeah, I could do it," Aaron said.

Taking down Jorge wasn't going to be easy. He was well positioned and Aaron was going to have to do it in front of Ramos. Who knew when Ramos would be back? Unless he went after Javier. There would be more opportunity and it would interrupt the flow, maybe give the team some time to put a tracker on the van they'd used. Right now, they didn't know if the teens were being moved every day or what.

"There's another player I can try for. But we are going to have to establish a pattern before I can do that. I'll keep my eye open for an opportunity," Aaron said.

"Good. I trust you. Denis is going to be at Mistral's tonight and Rick will be at the parking lot in the morning, watching," Jayne said.

"Lee, I need you looking out for teens being brought into the club," Hammond added. "Is there a chance you could set up some cameras in the hallways and at the back doors?"

Aaron realized that this joint operation meant he was no longer in charge of his own op. "She can watch, but the cameras are going to have to wait. I need to get a better feel for who's in and who's out of the place."

Hammond didn't like that and shook his head. "Without eyes—"

"Aaron's in charge in the club. We'll wait for your direction," Jayne interjected.

He smiled, glad to know his boss had his back, but Aaron had always suspected she would. "I will find a place. Just need time to see what's happening. Last night was different with me meeting the other players."

"Fair enough. I'm planting an agent at the coffee shop…Zara's Brew," Hammond said. "Also, I've gotten permission to put cameras on the streetlamps around the strip mall and the coffee shop. We'll keep an eye on what's going on outside until we can get eyes inside there."

"Give me access to the cameras so that I can flag it against the footage I'm already running through facial recognition," Lee said.

Hammond nodded. "You have total access to all the information we have. Did the missing girl you are tracking have a connection to any of the shops in the mall?"

Lee accessed her photo library via the cloud on her computer and clicked on the receipt. Then opened a second window to look at the shops in the mall. Looking over her shoulder, Aaron noticed the receipt was from an old till, the kind that was typical of secondhand or charity shops.

She painstakingly went through each store, finally getting to Frankie's Vintage Fashions. Zooming in on the shop, she hovered over the mannequins in the windows wearing secondhand clothes. Aaron could tell from the excited look on her face that she might have discovered something.

"There's a place that could be a potential lead. Frankie's," she told the team. "I have a receipt I found in the pocket of a jacket at Isabell's house. I'll check it out tomorrow."

"I'll send some undercover agents in too," Hammond said.

"No. There's too many new people," Aaron told him. "That's a sign that La Fortunata syndicate will recognize. Let the three of us do it. Rick's just sleeping in his car, but Lee can go in and say she needs some new clothes for this gig. She's new but known to the gang," he said. "Your coffee-shop person is the only new person I want there."

Before Hammond had a chance to argue further, Aaron went on to say, "We spent a long time setting this up, Hammond. We're finally close to catching La Fortunata and I think they might be part of your people smuggling ring as well."

"We believe they are pulling the strings behind the operation. We've only uncovered small players so far, and they don't have the funds to move the teens around the way they have been. Which means these kids stay gone," Jayne said.

"How many teens are missing?" Denis asked.

"Dozens in this area. Usually from the same school district or neighborhood," Hammond said.

"That explains why the cops are so blasé about looking for Isabell. What about the families?" Lee asked. "Are they usually gone?"

"Some are. We are getting about fifty percent reporting from teachers and the other reports from parents," Hammond replied. "The cops direct all of the cases to us to investigate."

"Do you think there is someone in the schools involved?" Lee asked.

Hammond raised his eyebrows as if to say he wasn't sure. "I've got two subs at the schools to see what they can find. But right now, we're not entirely certain. Your girl is from the same high school as several kids who disappeared."

When the meeting broke up he pulled Lee to the side.

"What's up?"

"I don't like those numbers," she said to him quietly. "Why didn't Boyd mention the other kids?"

"Sounds like he's hiding something," Aaron said.

Lee gave him a hard look. "I've known him since high school."

"So?"

"Forget it."

She turned to leave and he stopped her with his hand on her shoulder. "Sorry. I don't trust anyone."

"Anyone?"

"Well, you," he said, leaning in close. "Sometimes Xander and Denis."

"Me?"

"Don't make me repeat it," he said. "Call your friend and talk to him."

"I'm planning on it."

Aaron needed to be at the club before Lee and they'd decided to ride over together. She'd done her hair and makeup and put on the same dress as the night before. She was going to go into the vintage-clothing place while he went to the club. They hadn't had any time alone, really, until now when they were in the car heading back to Mistral's.

"You okay?" Aaron asked her as they were driving. She seemed distracted and that wasn't what he was used to from her.

"Yeah, why?"

"You don't seem to be all here," he said. "If you need a night off, I can make an excuse. You've had a rough day."

"No, I'm good to work. I'm not distracted per se, but

the connection between the school and these kids isn't one I was expecting," she admitted.

Her friend worked at the school. "Did you get a chance to call your friend? Do you think he knows more than they said?"

"Not really sure. It is interesting that he came to me with this girl after so many other kids have gone missing there," she said. "Hard not to think the worst."

"How so?"

She really didn't want to say it out loud, because then it would be real. Kind of like when she'd recognized Cate and tried to convince herself that possibly it couldn't be her. She didn't want to think the worst of Boyd. He was all she had left of Hannah… But Aaron was right there. Supportive and waiting. "What if he's working for the bad guys and maybe Isabell got away, so Boyd asks me to track her down?" she said hoarsely.

He put his free hand on her thigh, squeezing it to comfort her. "It's not out of the realm of possibility. Depends on how much her parents owe or took from them. But he could just be a concerned teacher too," Aaron told her.

Her lips quirked. "Playing devil's advocate?"

"Just learned through experience that you can't rule out common decency." No one was all good or all bad. Even if her friend was involved, he might genuinely care for the Montez girl and want to keep her safe. Working undercover showed him all the time the varying degrees that people were willing to go to. Everyone cared for someone. "So what are you going to do?"

"About Boyd?"

He nodded.

"Not sure yet. I'm going to go to the school and check

up on her friends. I'd already planned to do that. But I'll check on him too. Hammond will pull the class schedules for the kids who have disappeared. Maybe there will be a pattern."

There was *always* a pattern. Aaron knew half of his success came from spotting the connections and making the right ones. However, there were spontaneous coincidences as well, which could be misconstrued as patterns. He'd gone down the wrong path more than once. That was part of undercover work. No one was perfect.

"I'm happy to help if you need me to," he offered. "You're not working this on your own. I'll ask around and see what I can find out about the school dealers."

"Thanks. I'm worried about how much time has passed. If she's being held, then there's a chance we're not getting her back unless we can get into that house. Which even Hammond knows is a long shot. That's why he was so keen on your boss pressing you to get moved there." She shot him a warning look. "You can't trust Hammond… I mean, not with yourself. He'll always put the mission first. He's single-minded when it comes to stopping trafficking and he'll throw you under the bus to do it."

Aaron wanted to ask her more about that but wasn't sure if the timing was right. But in the end, he couldn't hold off. "You worked for him, right?"

"Yeah. What do you want to know?" she asked.

"What happened, but I'm not sure we have time before we get to Mistral's," he admitted.

"I'm not sure I want to tell you."

"Fair enough. But it's tied to the woman you thought was Cate?"

"It is. If she is in fact Cate, she's dangerous. We suspect she is the daughter of the head of La Fortunata syndicate, raised separately from Perses and brought up with no connections so she could infiltrate the FBI and become a mole. She gave them the entire operation that we used to have." Lee blew out a breath. "She didn't just burn me and Van, she shook Hammond to the core. He wants her."

"You and Van do too," he said quietly.

"We do. I hope you never have to experience it, Aaron, but when someone betrays your cover it feels *personal*. I don't know how I couldn't see past the role Cate was playing. It made me second-guess myself for a long time," she admitted.

He squeezed her thigh as he turned into the parking lot of the strip mall where Mistral's was. "It's in our nature to trust people we have a bond with. That's why working undercover is so successful. Everyone is looking for another person who sees the world the way they do."

She put her hand on his and rubbed his knuckles where he had a thick scar from cutting his hand when he'd punched a window as a sixteen-year-old boy. It had bled like a mother and hurt like a bitch, but he hadn't flinched or reacted to it. Just took it like a man. Which was the dumbest sentiment he'd ever heard. How did that prove anything except that he was stupid?

He shook his head. "We all make mistakes."

"We do, but mine and Hammond's cost lives. I can't do that again," she said. "This scar looks old."

"It is." He didn't want to talk about it so he kept the focus on her. "You *won't* do it again," he said.

"How can you be so certain when I'm not?" she asked as he pulled into a parking space and turned off the car.

"You're not a woman to make the same mistake twice. That's why you're tracking down this girl and that's why you're going to investigate your friend. You don't trust easily and you're not afraid to change your opinion of someone. A lot of people are."

"You're not."

"No, but then I tend to see the worst in everyone, so when I change my opinion, it's because they've proven they aren't a piece of shit," he said. "Not a great way to live your life."

Chapter 14

Frankie's wasn't that busy when she walked through the door. Like most of the retailers that operated here she was sure they did a really brisk business earlier in the day.

"We're closing in thirty minutes. There's a fitting room in the back," the lady behind the register announced when she saw Lee.

"Thanks, I won't be that long. I work over at Mistral's and need a few more dresses," she said. "Can you point me to some? I'm a size twelve, not sure if you have a lot of those."

"We've got a pretty good stock," the woman replied as she came around the counter. "Though I'm not sure they'll suit you for Mistral's."

"Have you been in there? I'm Lee, by the way."

"Candace. A few times. My boyfriend, Pete, is a bouncer there," she said. "You might know him."

"Yeah, we've met. The first day when I was trying to get a job and he mentioned my wardrobe needed an upgrade."

Candace winced. "That's not like him."

"To be fair, I was in jeans and a flannel shirt," she said wryly.

"*Girl.*"

"I know. But they are comfy." Lee giggled, finding herself slipping into her undercover role. "Have you met my man, Quinn? He's just started running the club."

"No, but I might try to stop by later after I close up here," Candace said. "Here's the rack. Take your time."

Lee flipped through the clothes on the rack, looking for a similar dress and instead finding something that she loved for herself. Not for the undercover gig. It was a fit and flare–style dress, which was always flattering on her curvy body type. She took it off the rail and noticed it had a sweetheart neckline. It was made of a deep sapphire velvet. So not for the bar, but she wanted it and a quick look at the price tag told her it was within her budget.

She found a few more dresses that would work for Mistral's and then went to try them on. The velvet had no give and the size twelve was from probably the '40s, so not as roomy as the same size today. But she was able to get the side zipper up, and when she turned to examine herself in the mirror…she saw a different version of herself. In this dress, she'd look right on Aaron's arm when he was dressed in those skinny suits he favored. Maybe out for a nice dinner…except that seemed like a dream.

Not when they were undercover and everything was so up in the air. Who knew if they'd even be able to go on a date after this operation was over? She knew he might be sent to another location to infiltrate another gang. Another worry was that she was part of his cover, like he'd told her. And the cover always came first when working this kind of operation.

She was still getting the dress though. When she looked in the mirror and saw herself…she liked what she saw. This wasn't a version of Lee that she had ever allowed herself to be.

Only one of the slip dresses worked; the other one clung to her hips and she struggled to get it back off. She heard the door open, and this time, Candace greeted the person who entered.

"There's a customer in the changing room," Candace said.

Lee hurried to get back into her own clothes and used the camera on her phone to try to see who Candace was talking to. A tall redheaded woman with her back to the dressing rooms. *Was it Cate?*

Lee swallowed hard. Unsure if she should go out there to find out. If it was Cate, and she recognized Lee, then Aaron was in danger. And she might put the entire operation in jeopardy.

Candace's face as she looked up at the woman's was tense, and she nodded a few times before reaching under the counter and handing something to her. The redhead took it and put it in her bag before walking out of the shop. Lee put her phone away and then left the dressing room area.

She noticed Candace was slightly paler than before but smiled at Lee when she saw her. "Find anything? Oh, that blue dress is divine!"

"It is and I'm taking it even if I only wear it at home. I'm also getting this dress," she said, holding it up before laying both garments she was going to purchase on the counter. "Was there someone else in the shop?"

"Just a regular who checks to see if I get any Prada stilettos in a size six. She comes in pretty much every week," Candace replied.

"Do you get a lot of luxury brands and high-end customers?" she asked casually. All the while thinking about Isabell, who was definitely not buying high-end. But Lee didn't have a receipt yet so she couldn't pinpoint this vintage shop as the place the missing girl had been.

"No, definitely not. I mean, you've looked at the racks. I get a lot of old vintage stuff more than Prada or Dior. My clientele consists mostly of a lot of teens and gals in their early twenties who have a good eye for clothes and are watching their budget."

"That makes sense," Lee said. Candace rang up the dresses while Lee toyed with showing her a picture of Isabell. But right now, she couldn't rule out that Candace was part of the operation.

The redhead had definitely picked something up from her. But what?

Candace put the dresses in a brown bag stamped with the Frankie's logo and handed her a receipt. One glance confirmed that it matched the one that Lee had found in the jacket at Isabell's house.

A zing of satisfaction went through her. She was getting somewhere with the case. Her gut had told her she was in the right place and now she had a connection.

"Thanks. Stop by the bar if you're in Mistral's later," Lee said, taking her bag and walking out of the shop. She used the spare set of keys that Aaron had given her to unlock the van and put her dresses in it. While she was there, she leaned against the side and texted an update to the team about the receipt and the redhead.

Pain and Panic were sitting at the bar when Aaron walked in. Both looked up from the drinks they were nursing, clocked him and then went back to their conversation. The bagmen would know all the houses. Which was why Aaron liked being one of them. But it was going to take time to earn enough of Ramos's trust to get that job. And these two were a team. He wasn't going to knock one of them out and take his place.

Or *was* he?

"Dudes. How's it going?"

"Not bad. You settling in?" Panic replied.

Aaron grinned. "Trying to. I like Mistral's."

"Everyone likes the club, and you haven't even been here on a Friday night. That's when things are another level," Pain told him. "Not that we get to enjoy it."

Pain reached behind the bar and hit the tap, filling up his glass, and tipped his head toward Aaron, who nodded yes, he'd have one. The other man went around the bar and filled up a glass for him.

"It's not always all work and no play. Sometimes we do get to kick back and have some fun," Panic said, handing a draft beer to him. "It's alright."

"Yeah. Maybe we can swap for a night down the road so you can hang here," Aaron suggested to Pain.

"Doubt that Jorge will allow that. We're part of his crew from way back," the man said. "Who do you know here?"

"Jako. You met him?"

"Yeah, he's alright," Panic replied. "You with his crew for a while?"

"Some time. Helped him with a problem and now we're tight," Aaron said.

The door opened again, and this time, Jorge strode in and nodded to Pain and Panic, who got up and went to follow their boss. The other man didn't acknowledge Aaron at all. Aaron left his beer on the bar and went upstairs to the office. The door was closed and he opened it with the key Ramos had given him earlier.

Though Aaron knew he wasn't the only one with access to this place. He guessed there had to be five or six keys to this door. However, the code to the safe was known only to himself and Ramos. So at least that was a bit more secure.

He sat down at the desk, realizing that he was going to have to start hanging with the rest of the gang. Getting to know them better. But that meant taking Lee with him and it would cut into the amount of time they had to go look into other leads.

Knowing Lee could hold her own in any situation didn't mean he wasn't still worried for her safety. Their cover was holding, but only a fool wouldn't know that it was tenuous at best. There were so many little things that could trigger suspicion. Sometimes it wasn't anything real. These guys were over-the-top paranoid.

His phone pinged. He glanced down to see the generic notification that he and Denis used, which meant that someone in their operation group had sent a text. Leaning back in his chair, he put his feet up on the desk and then used his passcode to unlock the message.

He was pleased with what he read. Apparently, Lee had spotted a redhead in Frankie's and verified the receipt her missing girl had was from the vintage shop. She also told him there was a connection between the shop girl and his bouncer.

Aaron closed his phone and got up. Time to meet the staff and start putting his stamp on the club. He went downstairs as more of the bar staff and bouncers were arriving.

"Gather up," he commanded.

Jorge was gone as were Pain and Panic. But Flo and Lee were there. Along with the bouncers whose names he hadn't learned and mentally was calling Tweedle Dee and Tweedle Dum. Plus, there was a staff guy and the VIP bouncer as well as the waitresses. All in total, ten people including himself.

"I'm Quinn. I've met some of you but not everyone. Tell me your name and what you do," he said.

"I'm Flo, I run the bar. Along with your woman, I have two other bartenders that work on the weekends, Marshall and Tyler. They take a few of the weeknights as well."

Aaron tipped his head toward the burly bouncer. He stepped forward.

"Name's Brian… I'm in charge of security." He pointed to three men standing near him. "That's Pete and Dan and Jack. We rotate between the front doors and VIP. On the weekends, I bring in three other guys who also spell us during the week."

"Jessie. I'm the head VIP hostess. This is Dana and that's Laurel. We have four more girls who come in on Fridays and Saturdays."

"Nice to meet you all," Aaron said, briefly making eye contact with each of the staff members. "For now things will operate as they have been, but if I see something that I think could run more smoothly, I'll mention it. If you have any problems, bring them to me."

Everyone either nodded or rolled their eyes and then dispersed to go finish getting ready before the doors opened. He noticed that Lee was back behind the bar, prepping glasses and her station. He headed over to the bar, leaning on it. "You find a dress?"

"Yeah. Found two actually. And met Candace, who is with Pete."

Aaron glanced over at the muscled man who stood inside the door, checking his phone. He'd start with Pete. It was going to take a bit to get everyone comfortable with him, but it was crucial he get to know all the players. He rubbed the back of his neck and then felt Lee's hand on his as she leaned over the bar and kissed him.

It distracted him from his own thoughts and he appreciated it. He would find a way to move up the ranks, he always did. An opportunity would present itself and then he'd use it to his advantage.

"Later, babe."

"Later," she said.

As he walked away he was aware that Flo watched his every move.

Flo kept her busy up until the time the doors opened. Lee had been hoping to find a moment to get a better layout of the entire club. She wanted to design some passive security features that they could use to monitor what was happening inside. But it seemed to her that there was always someone either observing her or asking her to do something for them.

"I'm going to be off tomorrow night and Marshall will be here. He tends to run late, so make sure you're here early," the woman said when they had a lull at the bar.

"Yeah, I will be. Quinn and I drive over together."

"How long you two been an item?" Flo asked curiously.

"About six months," she said.

Flo furrowed her brow. *"About?"*

"Yeah, he counts it from the first time we hooked up, and I count it from the first time we had coffee and I decided it would be more than a one-night stand," Lee explained.

Flo smiled. "Guys always think hooking up is a relationship."

Did Aaron? Hell, it was definitely more than a one-night stand, right? It had been for her. She'd learned early on that she couldn't control anyone else's emotions, only her own. "Yeah, can't argue with that. You with anyone?"

"Not now. This job is very demanding and I have a lot of responsibility here. So I have to take calls when I'm off, and it's a lot."

"Wow. Really?" she murmured. "My grandpa owned a bar and he was always fishing when he wasn't working."

"Every place is different. But I knew what I was getting into when I took this job."

Which told Lee nothing. "Will I have to be that available when I'm off the clock?"

"Girl, you already are. You're with the new boss and he's going to be pretty much living out of this place," Flo said.

"Do you do other stuff around here besides overseeing the bar?" Lee asked, being as subtle as she could.

"I do. I've worked with Ramos for a long time." Flo gave her a pointed look. "You'll probably be involved as soon as Ramos gets to know you."

Lee took that in. It seemed to her that everyone who worked here was part of the criminal gang as well. The last time she'd been undercover, she'd been in the command center watching over Van and Cate. But this time she was in the mix and it felt odd. Like she was out of control.

The rest of the night went by quickly and though she watched the doors she didn't see any teens in the club or going up the stairs. Aaron was the life of the party, circulating through the dance floor and mingling with all of the people in the VIP section.

When the club closed, Flo reminded her she'd be out tomorrow, then showed her how to make the deposit to take to the bank at the end of the night. "Marshall should pick up the bank for the register on his way in. When I'm back, we can work on getting you set up to do it too. Have a good evening."

"You too," she said with a bright smile.

Aaron was busy talking to Brian so Lee decided to check out the bathrooms and the hallway again. From her spot behind the bar, she hadn't seen anyone bringing money or drugs in or out of the club. She knew she was missing something.

But what?

Taking her time as she sauntered into the ladies room, she noticed that one of the stalls was out of order. Scanning the walls of the bathroom, she didn't see an obvious camera in there, but there was a mirror over the sink and she had no idea what was behind it. To be on the safe side, she turned on the hot water faucet until it steamed and started to cover the mirror. Then she went to the stall next to the out-of-order one, climbing up on the toilet to peer over the top. The "faulty" toilet looked fine and there was a crack in the brick wall next to it.

Glancing at the door to make sure she was still alone, she got down on the floor to crawl under the locked door and then stood up. She ran her hand along the crack and felt air stirring behind it.

Was this the outside wall? Mentally she reviewed the layout of the club. She was pretty sure this wall would be under the stairs that went up to the office and the locked room. But it was a *brick* wall. She didn't see any hinges to indicate a door.

She pushed on the wall and it budged. Not easily. So she pushed again and it moved a few more inches. The entire section of cracked brick moving as one. One more shove and a gap opened, big enough for her to stick her head through.

It was dark, smelling of dirt and a little bit like the club and bathroom. Then she heard the bathroom door open and froze.

Her heart racing in her chest, she waited with bated breath.

"Lee?"

Aaron. Thank God.

"Yeah. Sorry, won't be a moment," she said in case he wasn't alone.

"It's just me," he assured her, coming toward the stall where she was.

She unlocked the stall and opened the door. The water was still running at the sink, providing a fair amount of steam.

Aaron put his fingers to his lips, cautioning her not to speak, and she gestured to the opening she'd created.

He put his hands on her waist and shifted her to the side so he could look into the opening. Turning back, he whispered. "I'm not sure if this place is wired."

"Me either. I don't know how to close this," she whispered back.

He shoved on the wall again and it opened all the way. They noticed that it was a short hallway but couldn't see where it led. Aaron motioned for her to stay behind him as he used the flashlight on his phone to light the area up.

There was a door at the other end, but no one in the hall. He moved farther into it and Lee started to follow, but when he stepped over the threshold, the bricks shifted and started to move back into place.

"Wait here."

Chapter 15

Aaron was aware of Lee watching as he moved farther down the hallway. There was a door at the end that had one of those bar handles, and he pushed it open and saw the main parking lot, which was almost empty except for his van and two other vehicles. There was no light above the door and it was pretty much dark, but he wasn't sure if he could be observed or not.

He hadn't noticed the door and would have liked to observe it from the outside but still wanted to finish checking out the hallway. There had to be stairs if there was an exit leading out back, because there was no way into the club from the hallway.

He went back, letting the door close behind him, and only then turned the flashlight on his phone back on.

"Where does that lead?" Lee asked him quietly when he approached.

"Parking lot," he said, shining the light on the wall until he found cement-block stairs, which were narrow and not lit. "I'm going upstairs. Go back out in the club and wait for me."

"What if you need backup?"

"I'll be fine. Everyone's gone, but I'm not sure if

someone will come back. I need you to watch the club. So far, at least five people seem to come and go at will from here," Aaron said, coming back to her. "I'll be fine. Don't forget to call for help if you get into trouble."

"I'll be okay," she promised, then touched his face. "Don't do anything rash."

"I won't."

Watching her go, he waited until she stepped back into the bathroom stall and the bricks slowly slid closed. Could this entrance have been the one originally used to bring teens in? He wasn't sure yet. He knew that Lee would figure it out. That was her strong suit, he'd realized over the last few days. Give her a puzzle and she'd come at it from every different angle until she solved it.

He turned back to the stairs, not using his flashlight as he went up, because he wasn't sure what he'd find at the top. There was another door with a bar handle. Aaron took a deep breath, mentally ready for a fight when he opened it. He didn't have a weapon, but at his size, he didn't need one to deal with whatever he found on the other side.

He pushed the door but it was locked.

His adrenaline still pumping, he considered what to do next. He had kicked in a few doors in his time, but that would leave damage, which would alert Ramos and his people that someone had broken in. So that was a no-go. Then he remembered he had his keys, with a pickpocketing tool that he thought should enable him to open the door.

Squatting down so he was eye level with the handle, he propped his phone on his thigh, with the light angled so it shone on the lock. Then he started working. It took him longer than he wanted to admit until he heard the click and the lock opened.

Voilà.

He switched off the flashlight again and pocketed his keys and phone. Then, rolling his head from side to side, he cracked his knuckles and exhaled deeply before opening the door. When he stepped through it, he realized he was in the locked room.

There were four teens on the floor, all with their hands and feet tied together. They didn't even look up when he entered and he realized they were drugged. One of them sort of noticed him, but then their gaze dropped back to the floor. There wasn't anyone else in the room.

Fuck. Just fuck. Having suspicions, hearing that Cate O'Dell had been linked to human trafficking and seeing the evidence with his own eyes made him sick. He was on his knees next to one of the kids before he could stop himself.

Aaron couldn't free them without raising suspicion, so instead, he took photos of each of them and then took his tracking-and-communication device off his neck and put it on the girl at the end behind her long hair.

"I've transferred my device to one of four teens that are bound and drugged in the room at the top of the stairs at the club." Denis was monitoring his comms and Aaron wanted his partner to know that he'd left the device behind. He might not be able to get the kids out tonight, but he was damned sure going to track down where they were being moved to.

With his visual confirmation that it was teens being trafficked, the joint task force would be able to take action.

He left the room. Relocked the bar handle before going downstairs and exiting into the parking lot. He carefully made his way back to the bar entrance of the club. Then texted Lee to let him in. She didn't answer, which he suspected meant she wasn't alone.

Fuck.

He got to the door and had to pick the lock again. Which was slightly quicker this time. He let himself into the area behind the bar and took a moment to listen and try to identify who might be in there with her.

"You still have connections at Madness?"

Aaron thought it might be Ramos, and he was surprised because the dude said he wouldn't be back. Also was he looking for Aaron? If so, what had Lee said to cover for him?

"I know one of the other bartenders, but we aren't close," Lee said.

"Do you think you could *get* close?" Ramos asked brusquely.

"I can try. On my day off, I'll see if she wants to meet up for coffee," Lee said. "Aaron should be done moving those tanks around for me. Let me go check."

Before she came around the corner, Aaron walked out. "Tanks changed. Ramos, you need me?"

"I do. Let's go upstairs," Ramos said.

"I'll wait in the van," Lee told Aaron.

He just nodded at her. She gave him a worried look; now that he'd given his communication device to the teens, there was no backup if things went wrong. He squeezed her butt for reassurance on the way by.

After Lee left the club, he and Ramos went up to the

office. Aaron wondered if there was a silent alarm on one of the doors that they had opened and if his cover might have been blown.

From the moment she'd come out of the bathroom and seen Ramos standing at the bar, Lee had been on edge. She had no time to warn Aaron. Denis was listening, but he would only send in help when and if she asked for it. Which right now she didn't know if she would.

"Where's Quinn?" Ramos asked.

"I asked him to change the tanks for me. Trying to prep for tomorrow. Flo's off and she mentioned Marshall tends to run late," Lee said.

"You're Quinn's woman," he said.

"Yeah, came over when Quinn did. I used to work at Madness," she said, using the cover story they'd already established. She'd okayed it with Luna and Nick, so she felt safe mentioning it to Ramos.

"How long did you work there?" he asked.

"Almost a year."

"Why'd you leave?"

"Quinn said he'd be running Mistral's and we thought it would be nice to work together," she told him. Not sure if that was what Ramos wanted to hear or not. He was a big man with a buzz cut and tattoo sleeves on both arms. She noted he had something written in Spanish on his neck, but Lee didn't recognize the word.

He watched her but gave nothing away. At this moment, she had no idea if he was toying with her or just feeling her out.

"You still have any contacts there?" he asked.

She told him that she had a friend that she wasn't

close to, figuring she'd use Luna if she needed to. Then he asked her to try to get closer.

She guessed he wanted a connection in that club. Nick ran a tight ship, so there wasn't a chance for Ramos or his gang selling in there. Aaron came back, and he and Ramos went upstairs. She left and went back to the van, very nervous for Aaron.

When she got into the vehicle, she jumped out of her skin when Denis said quietly, "I'm here. Just get on your phone and act normal."

She shifted her hair forward, so if anyone was watching from the side, they wouldn't see her talking. "I'll try. Ramos took Aaron upstairs."

"Yeah, I heard. There are four teens in the locked room. Aaron left his device with them. So far, there hasn't been any noise in the room. But I have the team back at the office monitoring it. We are going to track them when they are moved tomorrow. Might be the same house that Rick followed them to yesterday. Not sure."

Lee was horrified but not surprised. As soon as she'd glimpsed Cate O'Dell, she'd known in her gut that kids were in danger. The information would be helpful as much as she wished she'd been wrong. She opened the app she'd created on her phone to double-check the device was still sending a signal so she would be able to monitor the movements. It took her a few minutes, but she'd already connected wirelessly to both her and Aaron's device, so she would be able to listen back and search for anything she missed while working.

"I've got it here. I'll monitor as well," she said. "Did you see Ramos enter?"

"Yes. He went in about a minute before you came out of the bathroom. He drove up in a Chrysler 300 SRT8 and his driver is still sitting in the car. Not sure if there is anyone else in the vehicle."

"When did you get in the van?" she asked.

"After I left the club. There wasn't anyone watching."

Good to know that he had gotten in undetected, but that brought another question to mind. "Where's your car?"

"Jessie came and got it earlier so I could stick around."

"Who's Jessie?" Lee was very aware that she was asking questions to keep the conversation going so she didn't have to dwell on Aaron by himself with no listening device in the club with a very dangerous man.

"My girlfriend."

She nodded and then looked back down at the phone. She saw the pictures that Aaron had sent of the four teens. They looked so young sitting against the wall. It almost seemed as if they were sleeping, but she knew they were drugged. Two of them had cuts on their face and necks. And one had a bloodied lip.

Safe to say, they hadn't gone willingly.

"I'll run the kids' faces and see if I can identify them," she told Denis.

"Thanks. That'd be great. I'm giving Aaron five more minutes and then I'm going in."

"I'll go too. Just need a weapon," she said. Relieved to hear that Denis wasn't going to just leave Aaron in there alone.

"Aaron's should be in the glove box. Use the key to open it."

She nodded. Denis was tapping something on his

phone and Lee got to work putting the teens' pictures into her database. It started searching and kicked back Snapchat accounts on all of them. She traced it back further and got names, then felt sick when she realized they all attended local high schools, one of them San Pedro High. Boyd's school. Isabell's school. What was going on there?

Tomorrow she was going to pay Boyd a visit and get some answers.

"We've got the go-ahead to go back inside. I'll follow behind you. I need you to be sort of whiny, like it's getting late and you want to go home. Take this hoodie of Aaron's and put the weapon in the pocket. Depending on what you find, use the opportunity to get close to Aaron and give him the weapon and then dive for cover."

Hearing what Denis wanted of her made her hands shake as she unlocked the glove box and took out the weapon. She put it in her pocket and then took a deep breath and closed her eyes. Trying to get her head to the place it needed to be to do this.

She was nervous and scared, not for herself but for Aaron. He'd been up there with Ramos a long time, and she had no idea what she and Denis were going to encounter.

"How will you get out?"

"Side door when you open yours. Ramos's car doesn't have a view of it. I'll stick to the shadows as best I can," he replied.

"Let me go in and I'll call you if we need you," Lee said. "No use giving you away if we don't have to."

"Okay. But if I don't hear Aaron's voice when you get to him, I'm coming in."

* * *

Ramos didn't say anything until he was seated behind the desk. He leaned back in the chair and rubbed his chin. Just making Aaron wait.

He lounged against the door and crossed his legs casually to let Ramos know he wasn't scared. But, in reality, he was tense and ready for a fight. Had been ready for one since he'd found Lee in the bathroom with that opened brick wall behind her.

This gang was dangerous, more so than they had guessed when he'd been set up to infiltrate and try to get the identity of Perses. He was also angry and wanted someone to pay for those kids who had been bound and drugged.

"Jorge said you were palling up to Pain and Panic."

Aaron shot Ramos a look. "They work for me."

"*You* work for me. They work for Jorge. Leave them alone."

"What's the big deal?" he asked. Not sure why Jorge was worried unless one of them was a weak link.

"He doesn't like anyone messing with his boys," Ramos bit out. "I'm telling you to leave them be."

"Sure. Was just being friendly. I'm new and don't really know who I can trust," he said.

"That seems to be going around. Jorge doesn't want you poaching his boys, got it?"

"I don't have a team other than the club," he said.

"The club is all you need. You stick with the club and keep everything running smoothly and we'll be okay."

Aaron shrugged and nodded. He had no issue with that for now.

"I want to get a toehold into Madness," Ramos informed him, switching gears. "Encourage your woman to use her connections there."

"No problem. I'll get her on it." Aaron knew Quinn would be the kind of man who'd make his girlfriend do what he wanted. Aaron not so much. But this was the business of living undercover. He had to play that part. Be someone that he knew wasn't true to himself.

Usually it didn't bother him, but this time, he wasn't sure. It was starting to wear on him in a way that it hadn't before. "That all?"

"No," the other man answered. "I heard you had some problems with Javier."

"Not really. Just walked out into the hallway after I thought it was empty and he was there."

"Watch yourself," Ramos warned. "Anyway, how did you think the club was tonight?"

"Not bad. One altercation, which Pete handled. I was hoping to wade in, but he didn't need me."

"You a fighter?"

Aaron shrugged. "Only if I have to."

"And you often have to?"

"Not all the time. I don't look for trouble, but if it finds me, then I'm happy to oblige," Aaron replied. Knowing that wasn't a lie. That part of Quinn was totally him. He had no problem when things got physical. He liked to test his strength and a part of him was always ready to prove he was the alpha.

"Babe! I'm tired. Where are you?" Lee's voice came up the stairs.

Ramos raised both eyebrows at him, then tilted his head to the door. "Remember what I said."

Aaron nodded, opening the door and heading down

the stairs as Lee was coming up. She had his hoodie on over her dress, and as soon as he got close, she pressed the pocket of the hoodie with a weapon against him.

"I told you to wait in the van," he snapped. "You're embarrassing me in front of my boss."

"It's cold and I'm tired," she said in a sort of whiny tone that he'd never heard her use before.

"Believe me, babe. I'll warm you up when we get home."

"Are we leaving now?"

"Yeah. But next time stay in the van," he said harshly.

Ramos had come out and was at the top of the stairs. Aaron wasn't about to get physical with Lee, but he did take her wrist in his hand and sort of drag her behind him down the rest of the stairs and out of the club.

He noticed Ramos's car, and the driver was behind the wheel looking down on his phone as they walked by.

When he got to the van, he opened the passenger door and lifted her up onto the seat before slamming the door and walking around. Acting like he was angry. Anyone watching would definitely buy it.

He got behind the wheel and shoved his keys into the ignition, turning the van on and driving away.

"Sorry."

"Don't be. I'm glad you came in. But I had to be Quinn. I didn't hurt you, did I?"

"No. You didn't," she assured him. "Denis and I were afraid you were in trouble. He's in the back of the van by the way."

"Denis, did you get the message about the teens?"

"Yes. It's been relayed. The FBI and control agreed to leave the kids where they are for now. Tomorrow after they are delivered, wherever it is they are going, they'll access the area and plan a raid," Denis told him. "Jayne is pissed, by the way, that you took off your device. That's your backup."

"They were drugged and tied up, Denis. I had no choice."

"I know. I would have done the same. She's suggested you carry an additional tracking device from now on."

"Sure. Whatever. It's been a long night and I am spoiling for a fight," Aaron muttered. "Sorry for being an ass."

"You weren't," Denis said.

"Want me to drop you somewhere?"

"Jessie is meeting me at the gas station near your apartment. I'll walk over when you go in," he said.

They got back to the apartment. Aaron knew the other man would wait until they were gone before getting out. He went up the stairs to the apartment, aware of Lee walking quietly next to him. She hadn't said much since they'd gotten back to the van.

He wondered if she didn't like what she'd seen of him tonight. She had to know that undercover personas were just amped-up versions of traits that were already inside. He didn't like that part of himself, but he knew it was there and worked hard to control it.

He wished she'd never seen it.

Chapter 16

Neither of them said much once they were in the apartment. Lee was still processing the change in Aaron. It made her uncomfortable to be around him. But she knew that was *Quinn*, not Aaron. He kept running his hands through his hair and finally put his hands on his hips as he turned to her.

"I'm sorry. I had to do that. Ramos was expecting it," he said.

"I know that. Don't ever compromise doing what you have to while you're undercover. I get that. It was just unnerving to see the anger on your face when you looked at me." He'd scared her. She never allowed herself to dwell on the fact that he was so much bigger and stronger than she was. And while she didn't see herself as a victim, his strength gave him an advantage that she was never going to match.

"I would never hurt you, Lee," he rasped. "I need to know you trust me."

She hesitated. More than anything, she wanted to but, honestly, wasn't as sure about him as she'd been earlier in the day. It was almost as if she'd been in some sort of dream state of what this undercover gig would entail.

Sleeping with Aaron… She had no regrets about that. She'd wanted and needed him with a fiery intensity that took her breath away. But leaving herself vulnerable to this complex man…? Well, she had second thoughts now.

"You don't."

She took a deep breath, wondering how to put it into words. "I trust you to do what you have to in order to take down Ramos and get to the head of La Fortunata syndicate. And I know you'll do it."

He closed the distance between them but stopped when there was a few inches left. "Of course I will. That's my job. But what about you and me?"

"Like you said, the lines blur. Aaron and Quinn are very different men and I'm still Lee in both situations—"

"Put a barrier up. That's how I do it. I take what people want to see, and that's my persona in the club." A muscle ticked in his jaw. "Can you do that? Get that Lee and Quinn might be toxic as a couple because they are in a bad situation but Aaron and Lee aren't?"

It seemed important to him that she see the distinction. Part of her did. She knew that Aaron and Lee worked and played well together. But she hadn't thought of putting up a barrier in her mind when she was in the club. Could she do that? Would it make a difference?

"Lee, love, please see that," he ground out.

She met his blue gaze and wavered for a moment before asking, "Why is this so important to you?"

"I don't want to be the monster I used to be. I need to know that you can see something else in me," he said, his voice low and harsh.

One small step closed the gap between them and she

wrapped her arms around his middle, resting her head on his chest. "You are *not* a monster."

His arms went around her and his hand ran up and down her back. He held her to him but didn't say anything else. She hoped he believed her. Because as scared as she'd been by the change in him at the club, as more time passed, she was starting to see the differences in his behaviors.

"I just wasn't ready for any of that tonight," she admitted. "The last time I was undercover, I was in a van the entire time, monitoring everyone and everything."

"You're doing great. It was a lot tonight. I wasn't prepared to see those kids in that room. I knew what they were using it for, but that… It was a lot."

She squeezed him tight and stepped away. "It was. I have managed to identify them. They all go to local high schools, one of them the same one as Isabell did. I'm going to go visit Boyd tomorrow and push for some more information."

"Good idea. I was planning to see if Jorge will let me ride along with him tomorrow. Trying to build trust."

"That's fine. I'll be safe at the high school and you need to move up quickly. I don't imagine Hammond is going to wait to get the plan in place once he sees those photos. He wants the head of the organization, but he can't let those kids be used to get them."

He lifted a brow. "Do you really believe that?"

"I do. That's why he does that job. Depending on what I find at the school, I'm sure he's going to have an agent or asset who works for him set up there and let them get taken. He'll find another way in, once we know for sure what is going on."

Lee knew her old boss. The loss of those young kids when Cate turned on them all those years ago still haunted him like it did her and Van. No one was going to sacrifice those teens to get Perses. Not if they could help it.

"If Jorge says no, then Denis and I will tail him, but I'd like to get inside and see what the setup is like at these different houses," Aaron said.

They both went to their laptops and did a little bit of work checking in with their bosses and sending updates to the entire team. Lee was happy to see that Van was on assignment, so he'd be distracted from Cate still being alive. She'd always been good at watching his back and knew that she still was.

Aaron cracked his knuckles and then closed his laptop. "You want me to sleep on the couch?"

She looked over at him. *Did* she? "No. Do you want to?"

"Definitely not, but I don't want to push you either. Like you said, tonight wasn't what you expected and you might need time."

"Do you need time?" she asked.

"No, I need comfort. It always leaves me feeling gross and dirty when I have to really get into my undercover role, and those kids…"

She understood that. She felt the same way. Like everything good in the world had been sullied. She took his hand and got to her feet, leading him into the bedroom.

The night had been long and hard. A part of Aaron wanted to just find a way to get Lee out of this world and far from the gritty place that he lived in. The place that he'd made his own.

He wasn't even sure touching her was okay. He felt dirty by association, but when she pushed him down on the bed, falling down on top of him with her arms and legs on either side of him, he put his arms around her and held her close.

Burying his head in her neck, the scent of her shampoo strong in his nostrils, he closed his eyes and, for a moment, just held her. Lee had seen the same seamy side of life, and somehow there was still something good in her. There was a part of Aaron that was no longer sure he had that.

How could he be with this woman if all of that was gone?

"What are you doing?"

"Holding you. Keeping you safe," she said.

He tipped his head back so that he could meet her gaze. "Do I need to be safe?"

"We all do," she said. "It's really hard when you realize you can't protect everyone."

"A lesson we've both learned," he said.

His hands slipped down her back to cup her butt. She rested her forehead against his. "We have."

It was really hard to stay trapped in his own morose feelings when Lee was on top of him. Her breasts pillowed against his chest, her thighs on either side of his hips and her mouth so close that he would barely have to lift his head up to kiss her.

He wanted to kiss her.

"I'm not that guy that threw you in the van," he said. Feeling he had to clear that up before he kissed her.

"If you were I wouldn't be on top of you right now," she answered.

"Why are you?"

She closed her eyes. "I told you I'm not good at pretending. I like you. You're hurting and I want to comfort you."

"So, pity sex."

"Never." She got to her feet. "I'm hurting too. I need to feel like there is something good in the world."

She was looking at him. "I'm not good."

"You're not bad. You do the right thing in your own way. No matter the cost. And don't deny that you're paying the price from seeing those kids."

He scrubbed his hand over his face. He was. He definitely was. "I can't get them out of my head."

"Do you want to?" she asked. "Van needs to keep those images to hang on to his anger and determination."

"Your boss?"

"Yeah. He relives his worst moments again and again. Says it's his focus. I can't do that. That weakens me and makes me crumble."

"What do you do?"

"*Halo* with the boys sometimes. Manicures with Luna."

He put his arms behind his head, raising one eyebrow at her.

"We paint our own nails and drink wine and talk," she said.

"I use a punching bag normally, but nothing about this op is normal."

"No it's not," she said. It wasn't like she was just figuring this out. She slowly got undressed, not in a stripper, sexy way, just took her clothes off.

Aaron sat up and was naked before she was. He took her wrist in his hand, pulling her with him back to the bed. "I can't promise this is going to be the best sex we've ever had."

"I just need to feel close to you and know that we both are okay," she said.

They fell on the bed together. He rolled until she was under him. His mouth was on hers as she parted her thighs. He slipped into her with one long thrust, filling her completely.

He stayed there for a moment, not moving. Then he tore his mouth from hers, burying his face in her neck, whispering dark words of need and longing against her as he drove into her again and again.

She thought she wouldn't orgasm, that this was for him. But then there it was. Just out of nowhere. She arched her back and dug her heels into the bed to try to take him deeper as she cried out his name. He kept thrusting a few more times before he emptied himself inside of her.

He didn't say a word. She rolled to his side, keeping them joined together. He pressed her head to his chest, stroking the back of her hair.

"Lee."

Just her name. But the way he said it had her breath catching in her throat. There was so much emotion— need, longing, caring. She hugged him back, kissing his chest, telling him without words she felt the same.

Aaron got to the club just before Jorge the following morning. He'd dressed for a run in jeans and the hoodie that Lee had worn last night. And had his weapon tucked into a holster he wore at the small of his back.

"Mate, you mind if I tag along today?" Aaron asked when the other man came into the office upstairs.

"Why?"

"Just give us a chance to get to know each other. I'm used to being with a crew I know," he said, trying to reinforce the things that Ramos had mentioned the night before.

Jorge shook his head. "Nah, we're good. You steer clear of Pain and Panic too."

"Yeah, but why? We're all on the same team now. Unless you're hiding something," Aaron said. It sure felt that way. One of the things that he was always slow to remember when he was undercover was the fact that he wasn't the only one concealing stuff.

Jorge definitely had something he didn't want Ramos or anyone else to know about.

"You threatening me?"

Aaron put his hands up. "No, man, just calling it like I see it. The big boss might see it the same way."

"Not unless you say something. I just don't like strangers."

Jorge moved farther into the room, going to the safe in the wall as if the conversation was over. But Aaron wasn't backing down. "I don't either, so I'm riding along today."

Jorge turned to him. Frustration but also something else on his face. Fear? Maybe. Unease? Definitely. What the hell was going on here?

"Why? This isn't your job."

Good point. "Like I said, so we get to know each other."

"I don't want to know you. You're not riding with me, Quinn. If you push this I'm calling Ramos."

"You run to him all the time," Aaron taunted, realizing he was pushing the other man because he was itching for a fight. He needed to get rid of the anger and guilt and frustration that had been eating at him since he'd gone up those back stairs the night before.

Jorge turned and swung, clocking Aaron in the jaw and snapping his head back. But he'd taken harder hits. He retaliated, with a one-two punch, socking Jorge in the face and the gut before spinning away.

The other man came after him and they traded hits for a good five minutes before Jorge realized that Aaron wasn't going down and shook his head.

"You crazy, dude? You won't know where the houses are if you take me out," Jorge snarled.

"I don't give a damn about that."

"You just wanted a fight," Jorge said with a smile, and then he nodded a few times. "Fine. You can ride along today."

Aaron nodded back as he wiped his nose with the sleeve of his hoodie. Jorge did the same. They were both covered with bruises and blood from broken noses. Aaron realized that he'd needed more than the physical release of a fight with someone who was his equal. He'd needed to let Quinn out in a way that wouldn't scare Lee.

He'd said he wouldn't let her compromise the operation, but he wasn't sure about that now. Being this guy gave him a safe place to let out all the rage that was always bottled inside of him. But around her, he didn't dare risk it. Not just because he didn't want her to see him that way. But because it was hard to put that monster back in the cage. With Jorge, they'd created a bond.

He'd wager Jorge had grown up fighting the same way that Aaron had.

Neither man said much as Jorge emptied the safe after Aaron entered the combination. Aaron followed him down the stairs and out to the parking lot. He put on his sunglasses and didn't bother checking to see if Denis was in the parking lot; he was sure that his partner was.

He also knew that Rick was nearby with an FBI agent, and they'd tail the teens when they were moved. He took a deep breath as he stepped outside. "It's going to be a good day."

Jorge laughed. "Ya think?"

"Started with a fight," Aaron said with a shrug.

"Yeah, I guess."

Jorge led them to a black Camaro SS and they both got in. He tapped the screen with the built-in GPS after he put the money he'd taken from the safe into the glove box and locked it. "You can ride along, but you stay in the car at the first stop. They are really touchy about who comes and goes there."

"They?"

He didn't respond, just said, "Even Ramos isn't welcome. If anyone comes up to the car while I'm inside, keep your head down. You don't see anything. Got it?"

Aaron nodded. His gamble had paid off. Wherever they were going, it had to be someone high up in the Cachorros organization.

He and Jorge chatted as they drove toward Bel Air. Which fit with some of the locations they'd found Steve driving to. "Are you the only one who delivers here?"

"Nah, all the districts have someone. But it's just one person. No days off," Jorge said.

"You like that?"

The man shrugged as he turned the corner. "Yeah. This job is my life. My crew is my family. I'm good."

That was something he'd seen mirrored time and again when he went undercover. A lot of the thugs had no family and had found one in the gangs. They were fiercely loyal because the gang members were the only ones who had made them feel seen. In a way, that might be why Aaron felt so at home in gangs. He was seen not as one of four brothers or as the dangerous adrenaline junkie. But as himself.

His *true* self.

Which he'd fought so hard last night. He never wanted Lee to realize that Quinn was who Aaron was at his core, and Aaron was the mask he wore to try to seem more civilized than he ever thought he would be.

Waiting in the high school parking lot for Boyd brought back so many memories. Though, back in the day, Lee had walked to school and would have been sitting outside in the hall waiting for the doors to open.

The school was in the center of a busy commercial area with a burger joint across the street that looked like an old drive-in/diner.

Boyd pulled in on his motorcycle after students had started to arrive and took off his helmet, stowing it in the compartment under the seat.

Several students waved at him as they headed into the main school building. She got out of her car and headed over toward him.

"Boyd."

He turned, surprised to see her. "Lee. Is everything— Come to my classroom so we can talk."

He didn't say anything else, just directed her through the campus and into the main building and up to the second floor. There was a student waiting for him and he slowed down when he saw her.

"Give me a minute," he told Lee.

"Sure."

She leaned against the wall, watching him as he went to talk to the girl. Lee didn't even pretend she wasn't listening in on the conversation. There were too many connections to this school for her not to be suspicious of everyone who worked there.

"Hey, Mr. Chiseck. I didn't get the homework last night and wondered if you'd have time today to help me with it," the student said.

"Yeah, I have time after second lunch. Does that work for you?" he asked.

"Perfect. I'll see you then."

Once the girl walked away, Boyd opened his door and Lee followed him into his classroom. That seemed like a normal student/teacher interaction. Somehow that reassured her. But then again, she didn't know what was normal for Boyd. They only saw each other every five or so years when he asked her to look into a missing kid.

"Did you find her?" Boyd asked.

"Not yet."

"Then, why are you here?" he clipped out. "I don't have a lot of time before class starts."

Lee shook her head. "You didn't tell me there were other students who've gone missing from this school, Boyd."

"I didn't think it mattered. They aren't my students."

"It *does* matter," Lee insisted. "You only care about your students?"

Shoulders tensing, Boyd turned and strode to his desk at the front of the classroom. "It's not the way you're making it sound. Isabell started changing in the weeks leading up to her disappearance. I have no idea about the other kids. I think one of the other students… The principal told us his family had moved."

Lee didn't know about that, but it made sense. "Have any of them come back to school?"

"No. Lee, this is what I'm worried about. Something is going on here," Boyd muttered.

Yeah, something was… But how involved was her friend?

"Why didn't you mention that other student earlier?"

"I wasn't sure you needed to know or that it was relevant to Isabell," he said.

Her friend was contradicting himself. "What's going on here, Boyd? Don't tell me any more lies."

He shoved his hands in his hair and turned away from her. "I don't know. That's the *truth*. When the first kid went missing, all of the teachers were concerned and we spoke to the principal, who brought in the cops. They assured us they'd do everything to find him, but he often skipped school and wasn't the best student."

"So everyone assumed he dropped out?"

"Something like that," he answered. "But the next one was a girl. Honor student from a good family. They were furious and went to the commissioner and two days later her body was found by the side of the road."

That was horrifying. An image of Isabell dead on the

side of the road flashed through Lee's mind. Her heart thundered in her ears as sweat formed on her chest. She needed to find Isabell. Now. She wondered if he even knew about the girl that Aaron had identified last night. It hadn't been long enough for her family to report her missing.

"The next boy is the one who moved, Harry. So when Isabell didn't show up to class and her friends hadn't heard from her…I was afraid to go to the principal or the cops. I knew you'd find her."

"Do you think the principal is involved?" she asked.

"Who knows? All I've got to go on is that two boys are still missing and a girl showed up dead after her parents made a big deal out of finding her. I don't want Isabell to be the same."

She could understand that. Sort of. "You should have come with all of this at the beginning. Again, why didn't you?"

"I was afraid you'd say no." He scrubbed a hand across his face and released a rough breath. "A missing girl is one thing, but missing teens and something going on at my high school…that's a *big* ask."

She narrowed her eyes at him. "Is that the *only* reason?"

"What are you asking me?"

"Do you have anything else that you aren't telling me?" she prodded.

Boyd shook his head. "Daniella was the teacher of the first boy. We had a big fight at home about it because I said some unkind things. She got pissed at me for being insensitive and left."

Interesting. "Did you tell her about Isabell?"

"She knew and said 'that's karma, asshole.' She's not wrong. All students should matter, not just the ones who show up every day clean and ready for class. I know that Sam—that's the boy—he had a rough home life. I shouldn't have been so judgy about him."

Boyd seemed contrite, but was it all an act? She honestly wasn't sure. "I need all the names of the kids and their addresses. Could you get them for me?"

"Yes. Do you want to talk to Daniella?"

"Why would I?" she asked.

"She sees all the kids because she teaches PE and they all come through her door. She might be able to find a connection," Boyd replied. "I didn't see one with Isabell, but you might."

"In that case, then yes, I would like to talk to her."

"I'll set it up." He met her eyes. "Lee, I'm sorry I didn't tell you about the other missing kids. I was hoping there was no connection and you'd track down Isabell's family and she'd be fine."

Of course he was. Didn't everyone who lost someone hope that they'd just show back up? That their worry was misplaced? But with so many kids going missing from one school, something else had to be going on.

Lee was determined to get to the bottom of it.

Chapter 17

Boyd's estranged wife Daniella reminded Lee fiercely of Hannah. It was obvious she must have run track-and-field in high school. Healthy-looking and fit, she had her long blond hair pulled back in a ponytail and her skin was naturally tanned. It was clear she didn't want to talk to anyone associated with Boyd, which made Lee wonder what had happened between them.

"Thanks for meeting with me," Lee said to the woman as she met her in her office inside the gym. "I'm investigating the disappearance of Isabell Montez, and Boyd mentioned you taught all the kids who've disappeared. I'm looking for a connection between them."

"Yes, they were all students in my gym class. As far as I can tell, there is no connection. I mean, they didn't hang together and their parents run in different circles," Danielle replied. "So I think the only thing these kids have in common is that they've all gone missing."

"And the principal, is he connected?"

Daniella shrugged. "He wasn't concerned when I first raised the issue and then I'm sure Boyd told you about Grace."

"The honor student?" Lee asked.

She nodded. "After that, we've all kept quiet hoping that… I don't know. It's hard to explain to someone who's not a teacher, but I'm invested in these kids. So when I see one missing or sick or clearly in a shitty home environment, I want to help." She blew out a breath. "But the law limits what I can do."

"I think that's why Boyd reached out to me," Lee said.

"Yeah, probably. Also, he knew Isabell. I asked him to contact you sooner, but he wouldn't."

This was news to her, but she worked to keep her expression neutral. "I wonder why not?"

"He hates your connection to Hannah and yet that's the only way he can still feel her… It's complicated with him." Daniella sighed. "But after Grace's body was found and we were all freaking out, I guess something changed in him and he told me he was going to reach out."

"Tell me what you observed of Isabell, if you don't mind."

"She was bookish and not really into running but loved soccer," Daniella began. "I think one of the boy bands she follows likes the sport and that's why she was fixated on it." Her lips quirked. "That age is so interesting, like right now, I have a bunch of kids asking me football questions so they understand the game when they watch it because Taylor Swift is going to games."

"Do you think Isabell was trying to be like someone else?" Lee asked curiously.

"In what way?"

"Well, her yearbook photo is nothing like this one I found in her room," Lee said, showing the two photos to the teacher.

"Wow, never saw her like that at school. She usually kept to herself, participated if I made her, but that was about it. I didn't see her hanging out with any of the other groups of kids. And I pulled her records—I'm sure Boyd did as well—she was a good student. You might try to talk to Tess Long, her English teacher. That was where Isabell's grades were the highest."

"Thanks for chatting."

"I just want her found. I want all of them found. And not the way Grace was. I want them home and safe and full of teenage drama and angst. That's all they should be worried about," she said.

"I agree." Lee reached into her pocket, took out a Price Security business card and held it out to Daniella. "If you remember anything else, please don't hesitate to reach out."

"I will." She took the card. "I really hope you find Isabell."

After saying goodbye to Daniella, she texted her update to the team. Aaron had his notifications silenced, which Lee knew probably meant he'd been able to go on the run with Jorge. Not that it was surprising that he'd managed to pull that off. Aaron was very good at his job...something that she knew she'd do well to remember.

Tess Long didn't have time to chat but did jot her a note that said, according to her, Isabell's home life wasn't difficult and she'd never talked about running away.

Lee sort of groaned when she read it because she was no closer to figuring out where the teen had gone. That room of hers had been picked clean, so it was possible that she lit out on her own before whatever trouble her parents were in came to find them.

It might be two separate incidents. She needed to get to her computer and start inputting everything and searching for patterns—

She was jolted from her thoughts when she noticed the tracker on her phone indicated that Aaron wasn't moving. Looking it up on the map, she saw it had stopped transmitting thirty minutes earlier.

She called Denis to see if he knew what was going on with Aaron.

"He's on a bag run and went to a new location. I had to drop back and am now in a waiting pattern. How'd you make out at the school?"

"No link between the missing kids, but when they made a fuss over one kid, her body showed up two days later. Not sure if that's coincidence or something else. Trying to dig deeper. I'll keep working on that. Let me know if you need me for anything," she said.

They hung up. Looking back at the pictures of Isabell, she studied them closely again. Both of those girls looked like they were trying to prove something. In neither photo did she seem to be a victim, which made Lee hopeful for her chances of survival. Unless the girl pissed someone off and then she was probably already dead.

But how would she have gotten trafficked? Those kids that Aaron had photographed last night weren't easy to identify. But she had a list and only one of them was from San Pedro High School. Hammond was ready to raid the house after his task force member identified it, but he was also waiting to see what else they could find.

He wouldn't let those kids be taken any farther, but he was going to wait as long as he could to get the most out of the raid.

Same as Aaron, she guessed. It was all they could do. They weren't going to be any closer to shutting down whoever was going after these kids until they had a lot more information.

Aaron wished there wasn't a part of him that really loved this kind of day. He'd had a fight, and that always seemed to set him back to normal. There was no pissing contest with him and Jorge; they were both big guys used to being in charge and they both recognized that in the other.

But he also wasn't part of the pack, and that was apparent when Jorge told him to wait in the car. That wasn't something that Aaron was going to do. Even if he wasn't undercover. He got out as soon as the man went inside of the large mansion that they'd pulled up to.

The fact that the property was landscaped and had a large twelve-foot privacy fence and gated entrance was already setting off alarm bells for Aaron. He was close to someone. Maybe even Perses, whom they'd been working overtime to identify.

The mansion was a large modern structure. There was a bridge that they'd driven over, and he noticed that there were wading pools that resembled a moat surrounding the entire complex.

The house itself was all painted concrete and glass. There was a large blown-glass sculpture in the yard that looked like a cyclone.

Perses was known as the god of destruction, and the

cyclone seemed to fit that. His skin prickled in excitement. Was this the home of the shadow head of La Fortunata crime syndicate? The one who'd eluded government agencies for so long?

He wasn't sure what kind of security there was at the place but assumed they had cameras and that his moves were being watched. He lounged against the car for a few more minutes, looking around the property like he was bored, before heading toward the house. Scoping out his best point of entry, he wandered down a lush tropical path that led to the side of the mansion. He noticed a patio off what appeared to be the kitchen.

Aaron hesitated. Once he entered the house, everything would change. He didn't pull out his weapon, which didn't worry him too much, but still he was going into an unknown situation. His blood started pumping heavier in his veins.

"I'm entering the house," he said under his breath for Denis, who Aaron knew was listening and had his back. There were two people in the kitchen, clearly staff who didn't even look up when he entered. He took a minute to scan the room, making a mental note of the layout in case he needed it later.

Aaron spotted a butcher block holding kitchen knives near the stovetop but ignored them as he had a switchblade in his pocket. He moved into the hallway and looked left and right. It was empty. He took a deep breath as he stood there and listened, trying to figure out where he should go.

Then he made his move. Stepping quietly into a large foyer, he stopped briefly to observe a rotating statue of another Greek Titan—or rather that was what Aaron assumed based on his knowledge that Perses was the man he was here to meet. The closer he looked at the statue, the more he realized it was a three-sided statue of the same woman. *Hecate?* He was struggling to remember his Greek mythology, but that made sense given that Lee thought Cate/Diana was Perses's daughter. She was depicted as she usually was, clad in a long robe, holding burning torches and standing back-to-back. But the rotating statue revealed that one of them was holding a sword in each hand and the other held a lead on a large ferocious-looking dog that lay at her feet.

His team had thought Perses had taken the name to create fear in those he led, but he was starting to wonder if the family were of Greek descent.

Not the usual drug kingpin in the US. But if they were trafficking internationally, perhaps a former shipping magnate? All questions that Aaron knew he'd have to wait to answer.

Hearing footsteps on the stairs toward the right made him move in that direction. He waited behind some sort of marble plinth that was taller than he was. Watching to see who came down. The first man was tall, older, with a square jaw and a full gray mustache. His hair was salt-and-pepper and full, falling neatly to his shoulders. He wore a white linen suit and loafers, and he moved like someone who was used to power and control.

Behind him was Diana, dressed in a full white pantsuit, her red hair swept up in an elegant chignon. As she walked down the stairs, Aaron couldn't help noticing the resemblance between the two of them. Her eyes were set the same as the man's and there was something about the bone structure of her face that made him believe they were related.

Aaron stepped around the plinth when they got to the bottom of the steps. "Hello."

The man looked over at him, acknowledging him with disdain. "What are you doing in here?"

"Sorry, mate. I'm riding with Jorge to get a feel for the operation and needed the toilet," he said.

"This is Ramos's new man at Mistral's," Diana murmured, coming over to him. "Quinn. He's been on the job two days."

"Do you want to keep your job?" the man asked.

"I hope to."

"Then next time, wait in the car as you were told," he snapped. He gestured to the corner where an armed, muscled man, dressed all in black, appeared. "Take him to the bathroom and then escort him back to the car."

Following the bodyguard, Aaron was tempted to walk slowly, but he could tell that Diana and the gray-haired man weren't going to be discussing anything while he was around. Which made him wonder where Jorge was. He'd been inside for a long time.

The bathroom was neat and large for a downstairs loo. Aaron took his time opening the cabinets, and knowing it was a long shot, placed a listening device under the mirror and notified Denis that he'd done that. He also provided a description of the gentleman he'd encountered, hoping that a sketch artist would be able to utilize it.

He was back at the car a few minutes later and Jorge was waiting for him. "Dude, I told you to stay the hell in the car."

"I had to take a leak," Aaron said, shrugging.

"Next time, hold it. The big man doesn't like anyone in his place."

He got into the passenger side while Jorge climbed behind the wheel. "Who's he?"

"The head honcho. He's in town for a few days for a big shipment and you don't want him to know who you are."

"Too late," Aaron said dryly.

"You better hope he forgets about you. He's not someone's radar you want to be on. Ramos is already feeling the pinch of that collar."

"Do you know his name?"

Jorge shook his head. "No one does. I'm not even allowed to look at him," he admitted.

"I see." Aaron now had a clearer picture of why no one ever gave up the Perses guy's name or likeness. There were few people who had that information and fewer still who would be willing to talk about it. He couldn't help but feel like he'd made a big breakthrough today.

Jorge didn't say much as they made the rest of the journey, eventually taking him back to the club before they parted ways. Jayne had messaged him saying they were having a meeting of the joint task force and Aaron knew it was time to get some new information.

The conversation with Daniella sent her back to find Boyd again. She wondered if he might know more about Isabell's disappearance than he realized. Waiting in the hall until his class ended, she was strongly reminded of her own high school days.

It was easy to remember standing by her locker between classes, while Hannah was chatting with her about Boyd and their dreams for the future. They had been one of those couples who'd started dating in ninth grade and seemed to be really in love.

Lee had never really been much of a believer in love. Her parents hadn't been the best role models. And her grandpa had a girlfriend, but they definitely weren't in love. She hadn't seen any good examples of it until, well, Luna had fallen head over heels for Nick, she thought.

Luna and Lee had immediately recognized another survivor in each other and their friendship had been quick and solid. So watching her friend fall in love hadn't been easy. Love made people vulnerable. The one thing that Lee had always struggled to let herself be. She wasn't saying that she wasn't starting to get the feels for Aaron or that they weren't deep. Just that…she wasn't really ready for wherever they might lead.

But Hannah and Boyd had been ready and never got the chance to see if they could make it outside high school. Well, she assumed that was the case, because Boyd had no staying power in his relationships. But how much of that was due to the fact that his first love had disappeared all those years ago?

The doors opened on the classrooms and the kids started pouring out. Boyd noticed her outside and gestured for her to come in.

"How'd it go with Daniella?"

"Goodish. She did know all the kids, and like you mentioned, they don't really seem to have any connection," Lee said. "But I was thinking there might be something that I'm missing."

He scrunched his forehead. "Like what?"

"I found this Polaroid photo of Isabell in her room at her house and I can't place it. It looks similar to a geo-tagged photo that was definitely taken at a club called Mistral's, but this Polaroid isn't from there," she explained.

"How do you know that?"

"I got a job there and have been looking around to see if it was," Lee said. "Do you recognize the location?"

She handed her phone over to Boyd and he leaned forward. His hair sort of shifted and she noticed the all-star quarterback's hair was thinning. The decades since high school were there on both of them, but not visible unless you really looked. She thought about the fine lines around her own eyes, which Van called laugh lines but Lee was pretty sure were stress lines from late nights staring at the computer screen.

She noticed an odd look on Boyd's face and realized when she'd handed him her phone the photos had shifted and there was a photo of her and Hannah visible. She reached over his shoulder to swipe, but he stopped her.

"She was so pretty…"

"And trusting," Lee murmured. She'd always thought that Hannah had been trying to help someone who meant her harm. That was the only thing that truly made sense for her best friend to just disappear.

"Yeah, she was. So where's the photo of Isabell?"

Lee pulled it up and Boyd studied it. She couldn't read anything on his face and she knew in her gut it was another dead end. Frustrated that she couldn't get a solid lead when it felt like she had a lot of pieces of the puzzle.

But something was eluding her. She was missing some connection. But *what*?

"Sorry, Lee. What will you do now?" he asked as he handed the phone back to her.

"Keep following up on leads. I do have the names of the other kids... It's interesting that San Pedro has had four kids go missing in a short span of time." She didn't mention the kid from last night since he might not be aware of her yet. Lee didn't want to give up the fact that they'd found those kids.

"Well, one was killed and the cops think it might have been motivated by her mom's stance on the three-strikes-and-you're-out policy."

Lee hadn't heard that but would follow up with Detective Monroe. "But then Sam and Harry and Isabell? I mean...that's a big coincidence."

"Yeah, that's why I called you in," Boyd said. "You're good at finding people."

"Not sure that I am this time..." She looked up from her phone to meet his eyes. "Did you ever meet her parents?"

"Her dad came to parents' night. She was a good student, so we didn't have much to talk about."

At least one parent was interested in her. Isabell being a runaway was making less sense as far as Lee could tell. "Where was the mom?"

"Oh, they schedule the night so that sometimes two classes that a student is in might be presenting at the same time. She was in an English class, I believe."

So both parents were interested in Isabell. Why then was her room empty? The house ransacked?

Lee needed answers before she could move forward

with her investigation. Aaron was busy infiltrating the Cachorros and she wasn't due behind the bar at Mistral's until eight. Which meant it was time to head back to Price Tower and do some real digging.

She thought better when she was in her place.

But as she got in her car after saying goodbye to Boyd, and started heading toward the tower, she realized that part of the reason she had a clearer head there was that it was just *her* place.

Aaron had never been there. It was where she'd started the search for Isabell. Clear of any and all distractions, and right now she needed that.

Between working with Boyd and the memories of Hannah's disappearance all those years ago, and Aaron making her feel all the emotions she hadn't realized she was capable of, her mind was sort of a chaos center.

There was more to what she'd learned so far. She just needed a quiet space to figure it out. And though a part of her felt like she was running away when she did it, she wasn't ready to share this information with Hammond and his task force.

Or Aaron.

Lee was used to being very good at her job and lately it felt like she had been spinning her wheels. It was time to get her mojo back.

Chapter 18

Walking into the first task force meeting wasn't what Aaron had expected. Lee had been distant and at Price Tower all day. He worried seeing him as Quinn was starting to make her realize the potential in him for aggravated behavior. But she smiled when she saw him and motioned for him to take a seat near her.

Denis and Jayne were sitting on the other side of the empty chair, so he hurried toward it. Once seated, he recognized Van and Rick Stone and knew Hammond from reputation and the video call. His boss had sent a warning to him and Denis to not mouth off to him.

But as his gaze moved down the line, Aaron froze. Steve from Jako's gang was there. Their eyes met. Steve shook his head. "You were too good. I should have suspected you were a government agent. I thought you were connected to Perses."

"And I figured you for a Chacal trying to move up. You were going to be my ace in the hole," Aaron said wryly. "Guess I can't turn you in now that we're on the same team."

"Probably not," Jayne interjected. "Would have been nice to know about this op, Hammond."

Hammond just arched his eyebrows at her. "The same could be said of yours. But Perses has his hands in a lot of things, so we should have expected our paths to cross."

"He does. We know he is tied to the biggest drug gangs in the US. This is part of a multiregional operation," Jayne said. "What about you?"

"We're running multiple locations, as well, for trafficking. So far, we've found a concentration in border states and economically deprived areas," Hammond replied before addressing Lee. "So what did you find at the high school?"

"I sent the information that four kids were taken from San Pedro," she said. "Both of Isabell's parents work for a company called WINgate."

"What do they do?" Aaron asked her.

Lee turned to him. "Defense subcontractor that provides border security."

That was a lead that they had been waiting for. Finally a break to bring them closer to Perses. Though Aaron was pretty sure he'd met the man earlier today.

"Did anyone have a chance to run the description of the man I encountered at the mansion?"

"We did. So far, we haven't found a positive match but a few possibles. The thing is, if they are controlling the borders then his photo isn't going to show up on security cameras," Jayne said. "Right?"

Hammond nodded then looked over at Lee. "Did you find out what WINgate is providing?"

"It is biometric scans, and as far as I can tell, they control the repository of all the scans. They then screen for known criminals. It would be very easy to black out selected people, as well, and make them invisible."

"Easy, how?" Aaron asked her. Loving seeing this side of Lee, who was in her element talking about tech and using it to help solve this case.

"It's just a simple code. They would put in the faces that they don't want to show up. From what I can tell, WINgate is the US company handling our borders, but there are similar tech companies in countries around the world. So moving drugs, people or whatever they want would be controllable if they had leverage."

"Do you believe they do?" Hammond asked.

Lee shrugged. "It's too soon to tell. Maybe WINgate is the trial to see if they can get in and control it. Given that we think Cate O'Dell is working with Perses and we know what she did, I think, yes, it is believable."

Hammond's face tightened. Aaron wasn't sure if he was upset that she'd mentioned Cate or if he was peeved about the fact that this had been happening under all their noses. Aaron's operation with Denis was focused domestically, but he knew that Jayne would be concerned about the wider implications.

They had teams who worked the border, and if they couldn't trust their partners who were building smarter defenses, then the DEA was going to be ineffectual.

"That sucks. How do we find the people in WINgate who are helping them?" Aaron asked.

"We start with the kids from San Pedro. My guess is there must be someone else on the inside as well. But they will be harder to find," Lee said.

He was going to ask how she knew that but realized she was speaking from experience and what Cate had done to her and Van. "We'll find them. So what's the plan?"

"What *is* the plan indeed?" Hammond demanded.

"I can get some guys in WINgate… We've just started a corporate security arm, so I'll send them in to make a pitch and get the layout of the place," Van said.

"Good. Jayne, what do you need?" Hammond asked.

As the ranking government agent, he was sort of in charge of this entire operation and clearly felt comfortable in this role.

"Aaron will continue trying to get closer to Perses and Denis will keep his eye on the bagmen that are moving around the city," Jayne said. "If we disrupt them enough, they will get sloppy. They always do."

Aaron agreed. He'd experienced that in the past. The more that a crime boss felt like things were moving out of control, the more they started to move pieces around. "I'll see if I can stir up something else. It seems to me that they are transporting teens in every three days or so."

"So that gives us a day and a half to get ready for a bust," Hammond said.

"The Chacals heard there is a big shipment for the Cachorros coming into the port on the same day," Steve interjected. "You might want to check that out with your gang. I got the feeling that Chico's death pissed them off."

That was good information and Aaron would make sure he was there. "Did you suspect the gang was trafficking?"

"We knew one of the LA gangs was but didn't know which one so I was placed with both," Steve confirmed.

"Dangerous for you," Aaron said.

"Not until you came along."

* * *

Aaron and Denis were in a confab with their boss, so Lee and Rick went out to the parking lot together. She had been told to keep on doing what she had been. And Rick had already talked to both Jayne and Hammond.

He leaned against her car, putting his head up toward the sun. "Cases like this are why I got out of the DEA."

Same, she thought. "It's frustrating to learn that no matter how many avenues we shut down, the syndicates always find a new one."

"Sort of the nature of the beast. And this time… maybe they are using the kids as leverage."

No *maybe* about it in Lee's mind. "I keep thinking about the cleaned-out bedroom at Isabell's house. I thought maybe she'd run from a bad home situation, but Boyd told me her parents were involved in her life."

"Doesn't mean it wasn't a bad home sitch," Rick said. "But yeah, I'm starting to think the kids are key. How did they think they were going to keep that quiet?"

"Probably got a local cop as well," Lee guessed. She hadn't gone back to Detective Monroe to be on the safe side. She really hated this feeling of not being able to trust anyone. It reminded her so much of how she'd felt after Hannah disappeared and after Cate betrayed them.

Two completely different women and situations but that same feeling of helplessness and fury. For her, rage always made her irrational, so she was trying to stay calm and keep working the problem with a clear head.

That was the only way she was going to find answers…and the girl. But it was hard when they were in a meeting like that one. Learning that Perses was more than likely controlling the border biometrics made finding lost kids near impossible. If one of his gangs had taken them, those kids' faces were never going to pop up at any border. What if they had access to CCTV footage as well?

Then she remembered she'd been accessing a government database to try to track Isabell and her parents. She pulled her phone from her pocket to verify who controlled the database. A few minutes later, she shook her head. "WINgate has the contract for all facial recognition tied to the US government."

Rick cursed under his breath. "We need to stop that— well, you do. That's not really my area of expertise."

"No, but the port will be. Thanks for helping on this. I know it's not—"

"You don't have to thank me, Lee. We're *family*. Besides, I needed this to remind me that I don't want to go back."

That surprised her. "Had you been considering it?"

He shrugged, pulling a cigarette out of his back pocket. It was well-worn and he turned it over in his fingers before shoving it away. Rick had quit smoking five years ago, but she knew he struggled every day not to.

"Sort of. Bodyguarding is fine, but I miss the action sometimes—well, not recently between Luna, Xander and now you."

She smiled at the way he said it. "I prefer the quiet."

"I know. You doing okay with this undercover thing?" he asked.

"Of course." But her colleague just looked at her like he saw through that. The truth was, she *wasn't* okay with this. She had hoped this kid would be like the others she'd found for Boyd in the past. Runaways who she'd tracked down in a few days. But in this case, it was like Isabell was hiding. Trying not to be found.

That was it!

The girl *was* hiding. She and her parents must have guessed that the syndicate would use her to make them do something. "I just thought of something."

Lee raced back into the meeting room with Rick on her heels. Hammond was on his phone and Aaron looked up as she entered, from the other corner. He and Steve had been talking.

"What if they don't have everything in place at WINgate yet? What if Isabell's parents need to do something?" Lee asked breathlessly.

Everyone looked at her, then Jayne and Hammond both moved forward.

"Like what?" Hammond asked.

"Like the actual computer part. Both of her parents are in informational technology. Isabell's room had been stripped bare. There was nothing left in it to identify her at all."

"You're thinking they got her out first. Sent her somewhere to hide," Aaron said. "That makes sense. If she's gone, they can't harm their daughter to force them to work for them."

"Exactly," Lee replied. "So where did she go?"

"Do you have any ideas?" Hammond asked.

"I have this photo. I can't identify the background," she said, holding it out to share with the team.

Everyone studied it and it was Steve who figured it out. "That's a hamburger joint across the street from San Pedro High. The Chacals work the parking lot next to it. All the students and teachers go there."

All of them… Then how had Boyd not recognized it? Or maybe he *had* and he wasn't telling her. "Is there any place she could hide there?"

Steve shook his head. "I don't think so. But it's not far from the Old Mission Trail and there are a lot of hiding places up there."

"I've got some time to kill before I have to be at the club," Aaron said, winking at Lee. "Fancy a hike?"

"You bet," she said.

The Old Mission Trail had been created by the monks who had come to California with the Spanish during the Inquisition. They'd created the missions all along the Pacific coast. A lot of the old churches had fallen into disrepair and were now in ruins. But there was a nice hiking path that had different edible herbs and plants growing along the sides, thanks to those monks.

Lee and Aaron had parked his van at the hamburger joint, and he sensed that Lee wanted to go confront Boyd by the way she'd glared at the high school. But he'd guided her around the back and up the slight hill that led to the trail.

"How well do you know Boyd?"

"In high school, we were sort of close because of Hannah, but I don't really know him very well now."

"Hannah. That's your friend who disappeared?"

"Yeah. We sort of kept in touch and he still sends me a card every Christmas, and every five years, he's reached out to see if I could help out a kid who he thought was in trouble. He was usually right," she said.

Grabbing her hand, he pulled her toward him and

locked eyes with her as they climbed the trail. "So that's what you think is going on with Isabell?"

"I did," she admitted. "I will literally never trust another soul on this planet if he turns out to be a rat bastard who used me to try to find Isabell for nefarious reasons."

Aaron couldn't help laughing at that sentence. She had to be really ticked off to say that. "If he is, I'll take care of him for you."

She shook her head. "Really?"

"Yeah. I'm supposed to be a thug anyway. And I do like fighting."

"I've noticed," she said, withdrawing her hands from his and clearly trying to change the subject.

"You know the problem isn't that you trust people, it's that people don't trust themselves and they are weak and make dumb decisions?"

"It doesn't feel that way to me," she confessed as they reached the ruins of an old mission.

Lee paused and Aaron took the lead as they walked into what was left of the crumbling building. No one was inside, but they both spread out looking for any sign that someone had been there. Aaron moved along the left wall while she took the right. He worked slowly, making sure to look for any remains.

If Isabell was on the run as Lee suspected, she'd be trying to leave no signs behind. He noticed indentations in the ground in the far corner. Like someone had been sitting and sleeping against the wall. Getting down on his knees, he shifted the sand around and found an earring. He picked it up as Lee joined him.

"What did you find?"

He held it up and she gasped.

She pulled her phone out with shaking fingers and flipped through the pictures, stopping on a yearbook photo of Isabell where the teenager had her hair in a ponytail and was wearing the earring. "So she owned a pair of them. Let me see if they are super popular."

Lee leaned against the wall, tapping away on the screen of her phone. Aaron left her doing what she did best and moved out the back of the ruin to search for a trail. A few minutes later, he found one. This time there were no signs of anyone trying to hide their steps. It looked like the hiker had slid down the side of the hill. He carefully made his way down there and found a backpack along with two sets of footprints. One smaller, probably a teen or a woman, and one definitely larger, and Aaron's gut said it was male.

He grabbed the backpack as he heard Lee calling for him.

"Down here! I stumbled upon some things," he said.

She made her way down to him. He was turned-on watching her work. There was something inherently sexy about Lee. "Those earrings were from Etsy and no two pairs are the same. I think these were definitely hers."

"Great work."

"Thanks." She smiled, then lifted an inquiring brow. "So what did *you* discover?"

He held up the backpack and then pointed at the ground. "These tracks look like they came from two different people," he said. "I might be reaching, but those larger prints look like a man's to me."

"Boyd's?"

"We don't know. Seems like he wouldn't have hired you and then taken her," Aaron said.

Lee didn't respond for several long moments. "Let's look in the backpack," she said, taking it from him.

She opened it up, pulling out a notebook and handing the bag back to him. The first page had Isabell's name written in it and a sketch at the bottom. "This was hers." She grew silent for several moments, just looking down at the notebook, flipping the pages. She shook her head. "Isabell was hiding from Perses's people. She doesn't know who they are, but her parents told her to trust no one and to stay hidden."

"That's solid, so you can use that."

"Trust no one...not even Boyd? What if he couldn't find her? I showed him that picture yesterday and he didn't recognize it."

"Now you're thinking he did?" Aaron asked. His gut was telling him that she was right. That there was more to this than either of them knew. "Do you think he's part of Perses's organization?"

"I'm not sure." Lee sighed heavily. "His marriage is in trouble and his wife said he's been odd. So perhaps. I don't want to believe that Boyd would hurt a teenager the way that Hannah had been hurt. That he would be complicit in taking a young girl's future from her. But right now, everything is pointing to him," she said.

"Do you want to ignore it?"

"I can't. You know I can't," she said.

"I know. Like I said, people make dumb decisions sometimes."

"That sounds like Boyd. Maybe he's given up on saving kids to make up for the loss of Hannah," she said.

"Maybe he's stopped blaming the world and himself and started to blame you," Aaron said.

"Whatever. If he's involved, he's going to regret it for the rest of his life."

Chapter 19

The club was almost quiet for the next two days. Van and Kenji had gone to WINgate to try to sell them corporate security and had gotten a nice tour. The two of them looked the part and Lee wasn't at all surprised by the friendly welcome the men had received.

Kenji had also been able to slip a small routing device onto the main security computer that Lee tapped into from her computer back at the apartment. As she worked, Aaron was showering and getting ready to head to Mistral's.

The both of them knew that this gig wasn't going to last for much longer. A part of her wanted to ask him about the future, but everything with Boyd and his possibly working with Cate had thrown Lee.

She had thought she'd changed and grown stronger over the last fifteen years but turns out she hadn't. She'd just kept trusting the wrong people hoping they'd be decent. Had she done the same thing with Aaron?

He walked into the room, looking at her carefully. "What's up?"

She shrugged, not really wanting to answer that. Right now, she was in her head and that wasn't a good place to be. Not at all. In her head, it was too easy to spot that Aaron was a chameleon changing to suit his environment.

The caring, understanding lover with her. One of the guys who liked to fight with Jorge. The charming manager at the club. He changed his skin so easily, slipping from role to role.

She had thought she'd had a glimpse of the real man but now…she wasn't so sure. Had she just been fooling herself again?

The way she had with Cate and now Boyd?

There was no clear-cut way to that answer. There was only the doubt and fear that she might make a huge mistake by believing in someone.

As if her childhood hadn't taught her anything. She could feel the crack of her old man's hand against her face and his cruel laughter when she'd cried. Telling her to toughen up and be smart.

Looking over at Aaron she wasn't sure. She didn't know the smart thing to do.

"What is going on in that beautiful head of yours?"

"Too much," she choked out.

"Talk to me," he replied, coming closer. Smelling so deliciously yummy with his aftershave and just that scent that was uniquely Aaron.

She closed her eyes, forcing herself to picture Boyd telling her he didn't recognize the burger place across from the school's wall.

"I don't really know what to say," she said.

He arched an eyebrow at her. "Undercover getting to you?"

"Yes. It is. What we found at the ruins pushed me over the edge," she admitted.

"I thought so. We don't know that your friend—"

"Acquaintance," Lee corrected. The Boyd she'd thought had been her friend wasn't the man he was today. They hadn't been close—it had been Hannah's disappearance that had caused her to think of him as a friend.

Aaron ran his hand through his hair as he turned the chair next to her backward and sat down. "I'm sorry."

"Why? You didn't trust him."

"Because *you* did and I think there aren't a lot of people who you do trust. Because this might be connected to a woman who betrayed you. Because Tony says life isn't fair, but dammit, it should be."

She almost smiled. Aaron was cheering her up. A new part of his persona she hadn't seen before. Now she was analyzing him instead of just taking him at face value.

"What's going on, love?" he asked again.

"I can't stop seeing everything as a lie," she confessed.

"Even me?"

She didn't answer him. But the truth was there between them.

"I knew this would happen. We have to live that lie every time we leave this apartment. Lines get blurred. But I've been straight with you from the moment we met, Lee. You know me."

She closed her eyes, wishing it were that easy. That she could just say yes, she knew him. But right now she felt so low...so stupid for not having seen Boyd's play for what it was.

"What if I'm the reason that girl gets killed?"

The words were torn from her. The real thing that was going on just ripped from her soul and her darkest fears. "That's on me."

Aaron stood up and came over to her, pulled her to her feet and into his arms. "That's on Boyd and Cate— or Diana…whatever name she is going by. Right now, we are going to do everything we can to find Isabell before she's hurt."

"She was taken… Those prints—"

He put his hands on the side of her face and kissed her hard. "She's smart and she's strong. Boyd had to hire you to find her. That tells me that he was getting desperate. Tonight we are going to capture Perses and Cate and find the girl. I know it."

"You can't guarantee that," she pointed out.

"You're right, I can't. But until we know otherwise, let's not kill her off. Let's bet on her outwitting them again," Aaron said.

His words were finally starting to sink in. She'd let herself get to a bad place…no doubt because she was tired and so much of this case was forcing her back to the past. A place she thought she'd exorcised from her memories but it turned out still had an emotional hold on her.

"You're right. Thanks for that. I was just—"

"You don't have to explain. I get it. I've been there. Remember when I sent Obie into danger and almost got her killed?" Aaron mentioned the case that Xander had gone on to rescue Obie and to help save Aaron himself.

"That must have been hard to handle."

"You have no idea what it's like to be sitting in jail while your brother and friend are being hunted in a swamp. And I really have no idea what you're experiencing right now but we both can appreciate it and understand where the other is coming from."

She hugged him, resting her head on his shoulder and trying to steal a little of his confidence for a teenage girl going up against a known human trafficker.

Aaron didn't want to let Lee out of his arms. He wanted to keep her close, but the burner phone in his pocket that he used as Quinn was vibrating.

She slid her hand down his butt and squeezed before she took the phone from his pocket and handed it to him. "Life is calling."

"The *job* is calling. It's not more important than making sure you are okay."

"I am. Now. That really helped," she said.

He looked into her gorgeous brown eyes and wasn't sure if that was entirely true. His phone went off again and he glanced down at the screen.

Jorge wanted him to come ride along this morning. Nice. He was getting deeper into the gang and felt like they were starting to trust him.

"I'm going to have to go in early," Aaron said. "We are still waiting for more information on the shipment that's coming in tonight. Once we have it confirmed, call Flo and tell her you can't come in tonight. I don't want you at the club alone."

She frowned. "Why would I be alone?"

"Because I'm definitely going to be wherever this is going down," he told her. "I want a second crack at Perses."

"Fine. I won't go into the club." She blew out a breath. "I'll just work from here and then try to catch up with

Denis since he knows all the drop houses. I'll see if I can find a location that Isabell might be held."

"Good. Stay safe," he said gruffly.

"I'll be fine. You're the one I'm worried about."

He kissed her long and deep, groaning when he pulled back because he wanted so much more. "Love, I always come back."

"Make sure you do," she whispered.

He walked out of the apartment a few minutes later. It was the kind of gorgeous Los Angeles day that Californians bragged about. He put his sunglasses on and headed toward the van.

The traffic wasn't too bad and he was at Mistral's in no time. Jorge waited in his Camaro with a box of doughnuts and two coffees. "Thanks for riding along today. Might need some extra muscle."

"Trouble?" Aaron asked as he got in and took a chocolate doughnut from the box.

"Not sure yet, but I don't want to risk my boys," Jorge said.

So much for building trust. But Aaron got it. Quinn was tough and strong and wouldn't back down; he was the kind of man Jorge could count on in a tough situation. And Aaron also knew that as Quinn, in Jorge's eyes, he was expendable.

He definitely admired the man's loyalty. When they started making the run, Jorge relaxed and Aaron decided it was time to start digging for more information. They'd need everything that he could find before the shipment tonight.

"Do you know much about this shipment?"

"Yeah. Why?"

"Figured this is my chance to show Ramos what I'm made of," Aaron said.

"He knows. The big man mentioned you were at the house. You're part of the crew going tonight. Ramos said to make sure you were solid and ready."

So that was why he got the invite this morning. "I am."

Jorge just sort of nodded at him. "Jako and his crew will be there too. Your old boss vouched for you again. That went a long way with Ramos. He wasn't too happy that you were in the mansion."

"Can't help what happened," Aaron said matter-of-factly. He had zero regrets about it either. What he'd found at the house had changed what they knew about Perses.

"Don't do it again," Jorge warned.

He nodded. "Are we going back there?"

"Not with you in the car."

The run was pretty much a duplicate of the last one that Aaron had been on until Jorge turned away and clicked on a new address on the GPS. One that he hadn't seen on Denis's tracking map either.

"New place?"

"Overflow. Business has been good lately," Jorge said. *"Overflow?"*

"Normally it's Diana's house, but we use it when necessary," the man explained.

Aha. Diana's house meant that there would be kids there. Maybe it was on the map of locations they'd tracked the teens to earlier. This could be the break that Lee had been waiting for.

He hoped they found her girl today. Lee needed that.

She was working hard to find Isabell, and the connection between her and WINgate was strong, so it might lead them to more than just the teen.

Finally getting a glimpse into this other part of the operation made him realize that this could be the break he'd been waiting for too.

He suspected that Denis and Lee were listening in and hoped they'd relay this information to the rest of the task force. Jayne had been clear that they weren't to lose focus on identifying Perses, and if possible, capture him.

Because Hammond was focused on the kids and human trafficking, Jayne didn't want them to let Perses slip away. She knew that Diana was important too and counted on Hammond, Lee and the rest of the team to take her down.

Their primary focus was the head of the international crime syndicate. Now that they had a rough sketch of the man, and for the first time in years of searching, an actual *sighting* of the man, everyone wanted him.

No one was going to be satisfied if he slipped away as he had so many times in the past. Aaron was determined not to let that happen.

The next time he saw Perses, he was going to stay on the man.

Jorge pulled into a neighborhood that had largish houses and seemed to be well maintained. A bit more upmarket than the other homes in the area. The house he stopped at had a large driveway that fit four cars and there were already two parked there.

The home looked ordinary from the front but there was a guy in surf shorts and sunglasses sitting in a lawn chair on the porch. When they got closer, Aaron noticed he had a semiautomatic weapon in his lap.

Denis stopped to pick Lee up in his van, which was equipped with computer and surveillance equipment. Between Denis and Jayne and the FBI task force, they had two sketches of the man that Aaron had described. Lee put them into the international database, searching for a match, and it was running a list of possibles as they drove toward the location that Aaron was at.

It was interesting listening to him without being in the same room. His conversation changed based on who he spoke to and how he wanted to be perceived. He'd sounded like a hired gun when he'd been in the mansion the other day. Lee hadn't been able to see the woman he'd been talking to, but having been the backup for Cate and Van all those years ago, she was more certain than ever that they were dealing with Cate.

Was Perses, the shadowy head of the crime organization, her father? They'd all suspected after she'd turned on them that her connection to La Fortunata had to be a personal one and someone very high up. It took a kind of deliberate dedication to give up a child and raise them to infiltrate the government.

Only someone who ran an organization like La Fortunata would do that. Or that was Lee's thinking.

Meanwhile, she'd gotten some hits on the kids and realized something she should have sooner. They were all members of a new social app that had launched about a year ago. It targeted high school students, and the registration restrictions were hard to crack. A new member had to scan their high school ID if they wanted to join. Then it was matched against the school's database.

The app had been touted as a safer online experience, making sure that it was only for students, and allegedly, it was monitored for bullying behavior. The back-end programming for the app was tight and Lee concentrated on trying to find a hack to get into it.

But she had the feeling it was going to take her more than a few days to do it. She looked at the developer information. Seaview Programs. She turned to her phone and used the internet app to search for them. The address was in Silicon Valley but when she used Google Maps it showed a Taco Viva.

"Anyone ever hear of Seaview Programs?" Lee asked in her headset. She was linked in with Denis and his boss as well as the FBI task force.

"It rings a bell. Is that the one that has that social app aimed at teenagers?" Hal, from the task force, asked. He was the computer expert and monitored all social media for online grooming and patterns between kids who were trafficked.

"Yup, that's the one. All the kids that have been taken from the same high school as Montez and the others that Aaron identified were on it." She hesitated. "Do you have a way into it?"

"It's hard to crack. I've been trying the back end," Hal said.

"I'm running that too. We need to get in," she insisted. "I might be able to get a fake ID."

"They run it against the high school database and so far no one has been able to grant us access to that."

"Hammond, you there?" Lee asked. Knowing her old boss was always listening in.

"Yes. I'm on it. I'll see if I can get permission today. Work with Hal on this," he told her.

Good. That was one thing down. She turned back to the sketch of the man. "Did we ever identify Cate O'Dell's family? That voice sounded like hers again and there is something familiar about the man in the sketch. Maybe they share the same eyes?"

"It did sound like her," Hammond agreed. "You have access to all of the old files. I don't recall that we got any further than La Fortunata."

"Which is a dead end," Denis said. "It all leads to Perses and we've never been able to get more than that nickname."

"I'm floating a theory that Aaron's guy is him," Jayne chimed in. "We'll have to wait to hear more from Aaron, but that guy didn't seem like he was reporting to anyone else. And Jorge sounded *scared*...or was that just my take?"

Lee concurred as did everyone else on the call that Jorge had seemed afraid of the man in the house. Was he the elusive Perses or just another heavy hitter in the crime syndicates? It was hard to know just how interwoven these gangs were.

There wasn't much for her to do but keep looking at the same information again and again. She had the feeling that she was looking too hard. If she could just relax, maybe the solution was right in front of her. But she couldn't ease up.

The chances of finding Isabell Montez alive and well were dwindling, and no one knew that better than Lee did. She rubbed the back of her neck and took a deep breath, forcing herself to move on to the next thing.

Cate.

A family connection, some clue that would give them a name they could search for. A name they could run against the face in the sketch. She opened the files and had to force herself to stay in the present as she read her own reports and remembered the woman she'd been. That Lee Oscar had been trusting and open. She'd thought her work was changing the world.

Having no idea that she'd been playing right into the hands of a criminal mastermind.

Not anymore. She was determined that this time she was going to find the missing high school girl, catch Cate or Diana or whatever name she was going by, and put an end to the crime syndicate that had been trafficking teens for too long.

It was a big ask and she knew it might not all be achievable, but she wasn't going to stop until she tried.

Chapter 20

Aaron followed Jorge into the house and the other man talked to the workers. There was a group of women in their underwear at the money-counting machines. A pretty similar setup to the one that he and Denis had taken down the day that Lee had come back into his life. It seemed as if a lifetime had passed since that day.

So much had changed and unraveled and then re-stitched itself. Which was sort of the story of his life. But now he had a new version of the tale. One that very much involved Lee. He drifted out of the main room down the hallway, which no one seemed to notice. The hallway was empty and not too long. There was a bathroom to the right, with no door on it, and the window had been covered over with a piece of plywood.

Typical of this type of house. He moved farther and tried the door on the left, but it was locked. Fortunately it seemed to be a standard type of lock and he turned the handle with all his strength until he heard it pop. He pushed the door in, scanning the room, and noticed that the kids he'd seen the other night were inside with about twenty or so others.

"Kids in the room to the left down the hallway,"

Aaron said under his breath and then stepped back into the hallway, closing the door behind him.

He was pretty sure, given Hammond's insistence, that they were going to get the teens out. But Aaron had a short clock to depart the premises before the raid took place. He went into the bathroom and flushed the toilet and then headed into the main room, where Jorge was talking to one of the guards.

"Ready?"

"Yeah," Jorge said, doing some sort of fist bump with the other guy before leading the way back to the car.

Aaron glanced up and down the street, noticing Denis's work van, and knew that his partner was no doubt waiting until Aaron was clear before raiding this place. Jorge wasn't talkative on the way back to Mistral's, which left him with too much time to think.

He had no doubt the raid would be successful, but what if that put an end to the trail they'd been following? There was a chance that this would spook Perses—if that was even who Aaron had met—to postpone whatever plan the big man had.

Aaron also wondered if Lee would find her missing girl in that mass of teenagers. He wasn't sure what the endgame was for the kids he'd seen in that room. Though he did know usually they were moved out of their home country to make them more pliable and afraid of running away once they were transported to wherever they were going.

Isabell Montez needed to be rescued in time. Lee wasn't going to be able to live with the fallout if that girl didn't. As much as Lee had seen in her career, there was still a part of her that believed good triumphed over evil. All the time.

But as much as he wished he could help, that was for Hammond and his task force to figure out. Getting closer to Perses was Aaron's primary goal. He'd gotten a good look at the different drop houses around the city and most of them lined up with the Old Mission Trail. Everyone was on edge with the big shipment coming in tonight. Which made an odd sort of sense given that most of the missions were ruins now and only accessible by walking trails. It was a nice way to move product without being seen.

When they got to Mistral's, Ramos was waiting for them and he looked pissed. He exploded as they walked into the club, punching Jorge and then turning to hit Aaron square in the jaw. Which Aaron countered with an uppercut to Ramos's chin followed with a solid jab to his gut. The other man was solid and didn't flinch but sort of stepped back.

"What the hell?" Jorge sputtered.

"The new house was raided. Were you followed?" Ramos demanded.

"No, we weren't," Jorge said. "I never am."

"What about Quinn? I told you to stay put."

Aaron rubbed his jaw. "I don't take orders that well. Jorge and I needed to know we could trust each other."

Ramos moved closer and Aaron got ready to fight, if needed, to prove himself in the gang. To let Ramos know that he might be the big fish in the operation but Aaron didn't bow to anyone.

Standing his ground as Ramos got closer, Aaron took a deep breath and was ready to throw the next punch.

Ramos shook his head and looked back at Aaron. "The big man wants to meet you again."

"*Big man?* The guy from the mansion?" This was the break he'd been waiting for.

Aaron felt the tension in the other man. He was suspicious of everyone and everything. Aaron had seen this happen before when things were about to break big on a case. Everything was unraveling and that made the situation more dangerous.

"Jorge, take care of the bags and get out of here. I'll see you tonight," Ramos said.

Jorge didn't say anything, just went up the stairs. After he was gone, Ramos tilted his head toward the door of the club. "Let's go."

Aaron followed him, not sure what to expect or what he was going to have to do. This wasn't something they had planned for. Denis and Lee were both busy with the raid and Aaron realized he was on his own.

Which had never bothered him before. But being with Lee had changed his thinking. She considered him part of her family now, and that meant that she might do something reckless if she thought he was in danger.

There was a part of him that cherished that thought, but he knew that it might lead to her getting hurt or killed. Which was probably why he shouldn't have started a relationship with her during this mission.

But it was too late to go back. He'd play the hand that he was dealt, and this time, he wasn't leaving wherever Ramos was taking him without the identity of the man in charge.

Lee waited in the surveillance van while the DEA/ FBI task force went in to raid. She was known to the gang who worked in the club, and as much as she wanted to be part of the group taking them down, she knew it was dangerous if she was identified.

She listened to Aaron bullshitting with Jorge on his ride back to Mistral's and smiled to herself. He had a nice, sexy voice and she could listen to it all day, but he was also clever at portraying the type of man that Jorge expected him to be on the ride along. Aaron was smart like Xander but he combined that sharp intelligence with a suave charm that his brother didn't usually bother with.

While she waited, she checked the progress of a piece of code she'd written to find any similarities between the kids that had all gone missing from San Pedro High School. There was only that Seaview Programs app as a connection between any of the kids, which left the not-so-apparent ones. Her first thought was that it was a fruitless search. The honor student's parents were a local politician and her catering-company-owning husband, the "dropout's" father worked for a cleaning and maintenance company, and Isabell's parents both worked for WINgate, which had a large campus just north of the high school.

She'd contacted the defense contracting company, which had confirmed what she'd learned before about both of them being on a month-long vacation. Which still made no sense, given the time of year. But that was the company stance.

She dug a little deeper on the politician, wondering if she had any connections to WINgate. Nope. Not a thing, but her husband's catering company staffed the employee cafeteria.

Lee opened another window on her laptop and put that information into a note. Then she checked on the maintenance guy and discovered his company was sub-contracted to WINgate. So all roads *were* leading back to that company after all.

Opening the feed that Kenji had placed in the WIN-gate security offices, she didn't notice anything and thought maybe they'd found her bug. All of the rooms were empty. Odd for the middle of a workday.

Then she saw Cate/Diana walking through the build-ing with two men behind her. They were dragging a teenager behind them. Lee leaned in as she hit Zoom, which made the video grainy but not too clouded that she couldn't make out Isabell Montez.

The girl had been found.

Lee didn't recognize either of the men as being Boyd, so maybe he had nothing to do with her capture, but deep down Lee didn't believe that. She'd been played by Boyd and maybe Cate again.

Lee was ticked off and ready to storm WINgate, but they were already taking Isabell out of the building. So instead, she tried to find the camera feed for the park-ing lot, then she noticed that two more kids and a group of adults were being moved out of the building as well.

"Something's going down at WINgate. I can't find the parking lot feed," she said into her comms.

She paused in her search, listening for the "all clear" from Denis. Originally she was meant to search for Isa-bell but the girl was at WINgate.

Aaron was making a joke about LA traffic to Jorge, so he was good. She went back to her search. All con-tracts awarded to WINgate would be public record so she sent a query and then waited for them to come back.

"I've got eyes on the parking lot," Van said. He gave the description and the plate number of the vehicle as well.

"Tracking it," Hammond replied. "Let them move. We'll make an arrest when the time is right."

There was silence on the comms. "You hear me, Price?"

"I heard you. I'm not going to let anyone get away this time," he muttered.

Neither of them spoke of Cate, but Lee knew both men were driven by their mutual desire to see her caught and brought to justice. There was a definite resemblance between Cate and Perses, and it wasn't a huge stretch to think he was her father. She'd always been close to her dad and had said more than once she wanted his respect.

Lee had been envious of the other woman, who seemed to have a close-knit family. Given that her own had been anything but. "How did I miss that Cate and her family were all criminals back in the day?" she asked Van on a private comm channel.

"We both did," Van said dryly.

"You're right, but the way she talked about it... Looking back it seems so obvious."

"Looking back, everything seems obvious because you know the whole story, Lee, but when you're living it every day you only see what's pertinent to the situation. This isn't on you. It never was," he said.

"But I'm the intel woman."

That had been her secret shame for so long. Information had flowed into her fingers from all places, and she was usually so good at finding patterns and uncovering secrets. How had she overlooked something so big?

She'd determined to never let that happen again but

she wasn't 100 percent sure she was achieving it. There were still moments, even now, when she missed things.

Like the WINgate connection. She'd had those kids' names for a few days. Was she once again letting personal relationships get in the way of her job? Was Aaron distracting her?

Van hung up and she went back to listening in, ready for some action, and then everything sort of happened at once. The raid was over and Denis gave her the all clear to come and help with the teenagers.

Before she could get to him, she got a second message.

Aaron was confronted by Ramos and is being taken somewhere.

Holy hell. Her stomach was in knots. Aaron could handle himself. She'd seen him do it so many times, but it didn't stop the fear that was eating her up inside. She had to stay focused. Help these kids first, then... Then she was going after Aaron.

The teens that had been rescued were transported to hospitals.

"Aaron's being taken to meet the big guy, according to Ramos," Lee updated Denis when he got back in the van.

"Come back to the office and so we can regroup. We can listen in on Aaron and figure out our next move," Jayne said on comms.

"I saw the sketch and am trying to run it through facial recognition, but so far, nothing," Lee told Hammond as they walked back to the van.

"He's stayed off-grid, so I'm not surprised. We're running it as well. I assume you're tapping into other organizations' systems?"

"I am. He's too big to not get a lead on," she said. "But I did also send a request for permission...so eventually the search will be legal."

"I don't need to know," he warned.

"I don't like Aaron alone at that mansion or wherever the big guy is," Denis said. "I know we need a plan, but he's a bit of a loose cannon on his own..."

"Want me to catch a ride with Hammond?" Lee asked him.

Denis looked uncomfortable for a moment and then seemed to make up his mind about something. "I want you to come with me."

Lee knew that Hammond and the rest of the task force were expecting them, but this was Denis's op, and if he thought Aaron needed them, she was going to trust his instinct. "Yeah, I'm good with that."

It made it easier to go along with the plan since Denis had been the one to bring it up. She was worried about Aaron as well. They didn't know the man he'd seen but Lee *did* know Cate. She might look all glamorous, calm and serene on the outside, but underneath that polished exterior, she was lethal. And if she suspected Aaron of anything, she'd kill him without asking any questions.

"Good. There's vests in the storage container, and weapons," Denis said as he got behind the wheel.

Lee climbed into the back again to monitor the listening device Aaron had planted. There was no witty banter with Ramos the way there had been with Jorge, and she wondered if Aaron was nervous.

But then she shook her head. That was the opposite of the man she'd come to know and love. He didn't get nervous. If he was quiet he was strategizing. She suspected he'd be ready for anything that he encountered at the mansion.

Being ready didn't mean that he'd be safe. He was still just a man, even though he seemed invincible, and she knew he could be hurt.

She wished they'd had more time together, wished she'd told him how she felt about him and hadn't been trying to keep the fake relationship for their cover separate from her feelings. Because now that he was going into an unknown situation on his own, it was painfully obvious that her feelings had been real from the start. That she hadn't ever been playing a part when she was with Aaron.

But then, emotions were the hardest thing for her to admit to. She could see other people's weaknesses and their bonds to each other, but for herself, she *hated* them. She hated how weak they made her feel. There was no denying that she was falling for Aaron and she was scared for him.

She wasn't sure what they were going to encounter, but she only hoped they were close enough to him when he got to the mansion. It would kill her to hear him in trouble and know that she couldn't help.

Hammond messaged that his border force contact said WINgate had won the contract approximately nine months ago. When the first kid had gone missing from San Pedro.

She called him back. "That's when the maintenance guy's kid went missing. I'm going to find out if he was issued a backup ID. He filed a missing person's case, but the kid was known for skipping school, so the police wrote it off as a runaway."

"Where are you?"

Oh yeah. "So about that… Denis thinks we need to be close to Aaron in case anything goes down."

"I always trust my field guys' guts. Keep me posted. We'll move in once everyone has been debriefed."

"Thanks. Will do."

She disconnected the call, and trying her best to tamp down her gnawing worry, started to compile all the information together that she'd pulled from the web and from Hammond. The patterns were all pointing to drugs and human trafficking and a way to make them both easier.

The San Pedro kids had been taken as leverage, Lee realized. And if the camera footage from WINgate was to be believed, Perses and Cate had gotten everything they needed from them, which meant that Isabell Montez might be dead.

Chapter 21

Aaron leaned back and put his sunglasses on as they sat in the LA traffic, heading back toward the mansion he'd visited earlier. He wished he'd had a minute to talk to Denis and Jayne. He wanted to know if they'd gotten any leads on the man he'd described.

Ramos didn't seem inclined to talk and Aaron wasn't sure what the right lead-in was to get the other man chatting. It was somehow easier with Jorge after he'd started that fight. It had broken the tension.

"You don't like me much," he said at last. In a way Ramos reminded him of his brother Tony, who just sat back and observed. Of course, with Tony, everything had changed when he'd become a paraplegic. He'd had to look at life differently and part of that was watching everyone else's reaction to him. That had been one of the many reasons that Aaron had struggled to forgive himself for the past.

These last few years, he was getting closer to moving on. Tony had trained and gone up Kilimanjaro last summer with a team. His brother hadn't been changed as much as Aaron had once believed.

"Nope," Ramos said in a short tone that didn't really invite more conversation.

Aaron looked around them at the other cars in the traffic. "You from Los Angeles originally?"

The man nodded.

It was too sunny here. He knew a lot of Brits craved sunshine, but there was a part of him that missed the rain and cloudy skies. Here, everything was too bright, too…well, it felt fake sometimes. Not lately. Not since Lee had started working the operation with him. But he didn't want to let his mind drift to that. He had to try again to get Ramos talking.

"Mate, we're stuck in traffic—"

"Listen to the radio."

Aaron flipped on the radio. The lead story was breaking news that a drug-and-human-trafficking house had been raided and more than twenty kids had been rescued. Ramos clicked off the radio.

"Wonder how that happened," Aaron mused. "The operation is usually tight."

Ramos turned that big head of his and said, "Someone got sloppy."

The movement was slow and deliberate, meant to intimidate. But Aaron just shrugged. He wasn't afraid of Ramos. He wasn't 100 percent sure he could take him in a fight, but Aaron knew he'd give it a good go. "Jorge?"

Ramos shrugged, looking back at the road. "He did bring you with him today."

"You accusing me of something?" Aaron asked. Was his cover blown? It was a question he had been afraid to even think as soon as he saw Ramos. But he was new in the organization and a lot of shit had been going down since he'd been moved to the club. Everything was point-ing toward him.

Ramos didn't respond at first as the traffic slowly inched forward. "Not yet. You see anything unusual at the house?"

Right now, there were two choices. Give up Jorge and make it seem like the other man was sloppy. Or… just stay silent. He was going to see the big boss so he wanted to go in with as much ammo as he could.

The team was listening as he debated how to answer. He was sure that Lee and Denis would be on their way to his location as soon as they could get there. So he knew he had backup, but there was also that feeling of being alone. That maybe this time he'd bitten off more than he could chew. Took one too many chances. Fate had been waiting for him since that cold, wet day playing rugby with his brothers when he'd hit too hard and hurt Tony. Had it finally caught up with him?

"I'm not sure. There was a van parked on the street when we left… Maybe they were watching the house."

"What'd it look like?"

"Standard service van. I think it was a pool cleaning service. White with blue letters," he said. Which was true. It was the one that Denis used when he was in the field.

"Could be nothing," Ramos said.

"Maybe. But the homes in that neighborhood don't have pools," Aaron mentioned. It was time to get Ramos's support.

The man did that nodding thing again as the traffic inched forward a little more. They were less than half a mile from their exit, but it was taking forever.

"You're good at details," Ramos said after a few minutes had passed.

"You have to be when you're the odd man out."

"How do you figure?" Ramos asked.

"The rest of you all know each other. I know the game, but I don't know the players here. I'm watching and learning to make sure I don't get burned," Aaron stated. Knowing that those words were probably the most truthful he'd given Ramos since he'd met the other man. There was an aura of danger around him.

He wasn't Perses but he was high up in the organization and Aaron could tell just from being around him that the man had sacrificed and killed to get where he was. They passed the exit for the mansion and seemed to be heading toward the port.

"I feel that."

"What can I expect when we get there?" Aaron asked. No use pretending he wasn't nervous about meeting this big fish in the gangs. He didn't even have a name, which increased his tension.

"Not sure. I got a call asking to meet you and telling me to get it done."

"Do you always deliver?" Aaron asked.

"I'm still alive."

Ramos's answer gave Aaron the information he needed. This was the man that no one said no to. It could have been from his earlier run-in or maybe the raid on a house that the gang had thought was secure, but whatever it was, he was now in the spotlight and there was no amount of talking that was going to get him out of it.

He didn't say anything else as they eventually got

off the freeway. Instead, he just started to get ready for a fight. It was going to take all of his skill, muscle and wits to get out of this alive.

The back of Aaron's neck was itchy as they were cleared into the port without showing any ID. Ramos followed instructions on his phone and pulled up next to a stack of shipping containers that had two other cars and a van parked in front of it.

When they got out of the car, Aaron bent to tie his shoe and relayed the plate numbers for the other vehicles to the team. Then took the small semiautomatic handgun from his ankle holster and tucked it into the back of his pants under his T-shirt. He stood, rolling his neck and shoulders, loosening up for whatever was coming.

His gut was telling him that the missing kids from San Pedro might have come to this big meetup in the van with the blacked-out windows.

Ramos watched him with a slight grin on his face before leading the way to a small warehouse off to the side of the shipping crates. There was a guy out front that Aaron recognized from Jako's crew. The other man lifted his chin at Aaron in acknowledgment as they walked past.

Moments later, Ramos opened the door and went in first. Aaron followed him in.

Diana was there, standing next to Javier, who worked for her, and two men he'd never seen before were with Steve. Aaron stared at the redhead, wondering what her part in this was. From what he'd learned from Lee, she'd used her spot in the FBI to learn the inner workings of the US government and their task force. That had to be a key reason why Perses had been so hard to locate and identify.

He glanced around, looking for Perses. Where was he?

There were four adults all bound, tied to chairs with gags over their mouths. Next to them was Lee's contact Boyd. Aaron knew that Lee wasn't going to like it, but she'd suspected he must be involved.

The teenagers... He immediately recognized the Montez girl Lee had been trying to find. She looked like she'd been in a fight and her hands were tied in front of her. Next to her were two boys about the same age. They had similar bruises on their bodies and were also bound.

"I didn't think there would be kids here," he said clearly so that Denis and Lee would know.

Ramos just made a grunting noise, which Aaron didn't know how to take.

"Quinn, Boyd tells me your girlfriend works for a private security firm and she's been investigating our operation," Diana said.

"WTF. She's a bartender I met at Madness when I first got to LA. Who's making the accusation? I'll take him out," Aaron growled, moving aggressively forward. Not giving away that he knew who Boyd was.

"I am," Boyd said, stepping toward him.

The other man obviously worked out and had some muscles. Aaron walked straight up to him and punched him hard in the throat. He used an uppercut to the jaw to send Boyd spinning backward.

Blood spurted from his nose as he fell in front of the teens, and Isabell kicked him as hard as she could.

"Enough," a deep voice boomed.

Aaron glanced over his shoulder to see the older man he'd met at the mansion. He wore a blue linen suit and had left the buttons of the shirt open halfway down his chest. Earlier Aaron had been busy studying the other man's face, but this time, he noticed the medallion and it was the confirmation that he really hadn't needed. A medallion of Perses.

Chapter 22

Lee was in a bulletproof vest with the rest of the task force as she heard the accusation from Boyd and Aaron's response. Aaron was good at what he did, and now that all the power players were in one place, there was a palpable energy within the team.

They were all ready to go in and take down Perses. Hammond's eyes were glowing with the prospect of being the one to crush him. And Van's were hooded. She had wanted to keep him from having to confront Cate again, but there had been no stopping him from coming along.

As soon as the sketch and grainy video from WIN-gate had confirmed Cate's identity, Lee knew her boss would be here. He wanted answers and justice. She got that. She wanted the same with Boyd. How dare he use her to find a kid to be used and exploited?

Jayne stepped to the front. "We will be moving in as teams. Denis and I will go first. Hammond and Lee second. Price's sniper is in position and the other three will be covering the side and rear entrances."

"Our objective is to arrest Perses and Diana and get the kids and their parents out," Hammond reminded them all.

"But we also need to know what the shipment is and where it's coming from," Jayne said. "So keep that in mind as we move in."

Lee nodded. She wanted answers too, and she wasn't going to rest until she got them.

"As soon as Lee walks in, things will kick off," Hammond said. "I think she should stay at the side entrance and I'll take Rick with me."

Lee agreed with the plan, and she and Rick swapped places. Rick was buzzing with energy but was calm as could be. She understood why he'd considered going back in the field. It seemed to really suit him.

The longer they waited, the tenser Lee was becoming. She'd only been on one raid before…the disastrous one where Cate had gotten away from them. Normally she was the eyes advising everyone where to go. But Jayne had a person on her team who was more familiar with all the players and the decision had been made that Lee would be on the ground.

Van looked over at her and arched one eyebrow. Lee nodded a couple of times to let him know she was okay. She might not have done this very often, but she was motivated to make sure that Boyd and Cate were caught.

"Move into position and we will go on my signal."

Lee followed Xander and Van around the building. Xander took the back entrance, Van the right. Lee was by herself, her comms on but silent as everyone waited for the signal. Aaron's and Steve's comms were being broadcast to the team. She heard the deep voice yell, *"Enough!"*

Then Jayne's voice came through. "Go."

"Guard at front down. Teams one and two are moving into position and breaching the building…now."

Seconds later, she heard the sound of the door being blown open and then screams and gunshots rang out. She was meant to wait and catch anyone who tried to leave, but she couldn't. There was too much at stake. She went in through the window that she'd been watching. Scraping her stomach as she fell through it. Then, rolling into a shooter's stance, she was on the move.

No one was alerted to her entrance. She scanned the room near her and saw that Aaron and Steve were both fighting with gang members. Boyd was flat on the floor and the kids and parents she'd seen in the grainy security footage were all bound and gagged, clearly frightened out of their wits.

Moving carefully and trying to stay to the shadows, she slid behind the boxes until she was close enough to the teens. She had a pocketknife and pulled it out so she could cut the kids free.

Tucking her gun into her waistband, she ran toward them. She worked quickly, freeing their hands, and then went to work on their feet. It felt like time was moving way too slowly. Every second counted, and when she freed the last kid, they all turned to look at her.

There was fear and uncertainty but also, Lee thought, a bit of grit in their gazes. She wanted to reassure them but with gunshots and fighting going on around them, she doubted anything she said would help.

"Go out the back door. There is a big man waiting who will keep you safe."

The kids took off without a second's hesitation, and Lee stood to cover them in case anyone went after them.

Cate noticed them and started to go after them, but Lee raised her gun and shot the other woman in the leg.

Cate fired back, hitting Lee in the side as she twisted her body and dove for the floor. "Cate's on her way out the back after the kids. Injured in one leg."

Lee knew that Van or Xander would get her. Adrenaline rushed through her, but the gunshot wound in her side burned, and she felt the warmth of the blood dripping down her side as she made her way to the adults, cutting one of the men free first. He took the knife from her and freed the others. "Go out the back."

The first man wanted to stay with her, but Lee pushed him. "Go! I'll be fine."

They hurried toward the back of the warehouse.

"Kids and adults are safe with Xander. Van is in pursuit of Cate and out of my sight."

Lee turned to try to find Aaron in the mix. He was still standing but locked in fierce battle with a tall, older man in a pale blue linen suit.

Perses.

Aaron wasn't giving an inch, but the man was built like Aaron, and the fight was too evenly matched. Lee was trying to find her gun when she felt the barrel of it pressed to the back of her neck.

"Stand up," Boyd said. "It's time for you to be useful again."

As soon as Perses stepped into the room, the air changed. Aaron looked over at Steve and saw the man had moved to separate himself from the other gang members who Aaron didn't know.

Aaron knew the team would be coming in at any

moment, given that Jayne and Hammond both wanted Perses. Meanwhile, he pummeled Boyd one more time, knocking him to the ground, and then kicked him hard enough in the head to knock him out. He pivoted to face the rest of the room. The hostages were all terrified, and the woman hostage was crying behind her gag.

"What's going on?" Perses demanded of Diana.

"Quinn's girlfriend is Lee Oscar. She was on the team I worked on with the FBI," the woman said.

"Why didn't you know that?" Perses demanded of her.

"I never met her while she was bartending at the club."

Perses turned toward Aaron and Ramos, and the guys from Jako's crew were all moving toward him as well. "You working with the FBI?"

"Fuck no. I'm a British citizen," Aaron said.

That didn't seem to stop them from rushing at him. Aaron rolled away to give himself some space before dropping into a fighting stance and moving toward the man closest to him.

The doors burst open as he did, and he saw Steve come to fight back-to-back with him. Ramos came straight for Aaron and hit him hard enough in the gut to wind him and probably break his ribs.

Aaron countered by kicking the other man's legs out from under him and then pounding him hard in the stomach while he was down. Ramos grabbed Aaron's leg and jerked him off balance, but he rolled into the momentum of his fall and came up in time to dodge a kick from Ramos aimed at his head.

Noticing Denis moving behind Ramos, Aaron hit the

other man in the face with a solid upward punch that broke his nose as Denis tased him and put cuffs on him.

"I had him," Aaron muttered.

"Yeah, sure," Denis said as they both turned to take on more of the men in the room.

In the midst of everyone fighting, Aaron noticed Perses making a move for the front entrance. He threw himself at the other man, tackling him to the ground. Aaron's entire body ached from the contact, but he ignored it, lurching to his feet as Perses stood as well.

A gunshot and the sound of Lee crying out made Aaron almost turn, but he knew better than to give Perses any opening. So instead, he pulled his gun from the back of his trousers and lifted it to fire at the other man, who was prepared to fight back. He backhanded Aaron in the jaw, making his head snap around.

Aaron was dazed for a moment, but instinct had him slamming Perses hard in the face with the butt of his pistol. He hit the other man three times before his head cleared and he was able to start thinking more strategically about fighting. He didn't want to draw this out. He wanted Perses down and captured.

Hammond was moving in, as was Jayne, and Aaron lowered his gun, hitting Perses in the kneecap, which took the other man to his knees. But he was still dangerous. His hits landing with enough force to knock Aaron off balance again, but Hammond and Jayne were both there as Denis tased Perses and they moved in to cuff him.

Aaron turned to find Boyd holding a gun to the back of Lee's head.

"Back off or she's dead," Boyd snarled.

Everyone stopped what they were doing. All of the gang members were in cuffs or knocked out and Jayne and Hammond were still next to Perses. Who was nodding at Boyd. "Get me out of here," Perses said.

Fear roiling through him, Aaron was weighing his next move to disarm Boyd. There was no room for hesitation or error. Never in his life had his actions had so much weight. If he made the wrong decision, Lee could end up dead. Something he wasn't going to allow to happen, now that he'd found her.

"Duck!" Denis yelled.

Aaron dropped as a bullet whizzed past him and hit Boyd in the forehead and the other man fell backward to the ground. Lee was trembling and pale, blood seeping down the side of her body, as Aaron ran to her. Pulling her into his arms as she fainted. He lowered her to the ground as emergency vehicles started to pour into the port.

He held her close, whispering softly in her ear. "I love you, babe."

Aaron knew the task force was taking care of the arrests, but he just stayed with Lee, riding with her to the hospital. He was checked for a concussion and released from the hospital but sat in a waiting room with Xander next to him.

It felt so much like that night when they'd waited for Tony. Hoping, praying, racked with guilt.

"She's going to be okay," Xander said.

"Yeah."

But Aaron wasn't entirely sure. She would recover from her physical injuries, but her emotional wounds might run deep. Lee had been betrayed *again* by someone she'd trusted. Aaron's hold on her was based around this mission, and the couple they'd created was fiction, but the truth was that nothing about his time with Lee had been a lie. He loved her and wanted her by his side.

What if she wasn't ready to hear that from him? Regardless, there was no other possibility for him but to try to convince her.

However, it might take time and Aaron had never been good at waiting. Finally the others from Price Security showed up, even Van, who had tracked down Cate and captured her, seeing her arrested.

They were all quiet, their concern for Lee was almost palpable, and Aaron wondered if she knew how much she mattered to this family she'd created for herself. And if there would be a place for him in it or if it would be better for her if he let her go.

Lee woke with a start in the hospital room. There was the steady beating of her heart on the monitor and her mouth was dry. She tried to sit up and someone was there.

Aaron.

He put his hand on her shoulder. "What do you need?"

"Water, please," she croaked out.

He poured it for her and handed it to her. "Take it slow."

She nodded as she drank and tried to remember everything that had happened. "Boyd?"

"Dead."

She had mixed feelings about that. She had wanted to question him and find out why he'd been working with Cate and for how long.

"Cate?"

"Van got her and she's being questioned," Aaron said, looking down at her with an expression that Lee hadn't seen on his face before and struggled to identify. "Perses was arrested as well and is being transported to DC for questioning. Your team is all here. We've been taking turns watching you and they went to dinner a few minutes ago. I'll text them that you're awake."

He reached for his phone, but she stopped him with her hand on his wrist. "Are you okay?"

"Yeah. A concussion and broken ribs, but that's nothing new for me. This hard head has saved me more than once," he said. "Why didn't you wait outside?"

"I was needed inside. Those kids and their parents had seen enough… Are they okay? God, I can't believe I didn't ask about them."

Leaning closer, Aaron gently brushed his hand over her forehead. "You wanted to make sure the danger was gone first. They are all good. Some minor injuries and they are all being debriefed. They had been forced to work for Cate and make adjustments to the biometric software. The kids were used for leverage."

"And Isabell?"

"Her parents caught on to what was happening and told her to be on her guard. According to Isabell, Mr. Chiseck tried to get her to go somewhere off school property with him, which creeped her out. When she told her parents, they gave her cash and told her to hide on the Old Mission Trail until she heard from them."

"Good for them. I was worried they were abusing her and that had made her run away." Lee sighed. "So she was fine until Boyd asked me to find her?"

"Yes and no. Her parents were taken and the house

ransacked, so Isabell was scared but sticking to the plan. When you showed Boyd the picture, it was all he needed to search the hills behind the burger place. He was the one who found her."

"I can't believe Boyd would do something like this," Lee said, tears filling her eyes. "Do we know why?"

"He had a lot of debt from online gambling, according to Daniella. She suspects he did it for the money," Aaron told her. "We might get more from Cate when they are done interrogating her."

"Maybe. She can be very tight-lipped, but then again, Hammond can be very persuasive," Lee said.

She sort of drifted off and when she woke again, Van and Luna were in the room.

"Hey, you awake?" Van asked.

"I am. You okay?"

"I'm not the one in a hospital bed," he said as Luna handed her some water to drink.

She took the cup and drank it as Luna helped her raise her bed up to sit. "Where's Aaron?"

"In the hall. He went for a debrief and has been here since. Said he won't go home until you do," Van said.

Now that she knew Isabell was safe and Cate and Perses had been arrested, she felt like she could finally breathe and think about the future. A future she wanted with Aaron, but he was an undercover man who moved around the country going where the DEA needed him.

She sensed that Van wasn't ready to talk about Cate and Lee was okay with that. She wanted to talk to Aaron and find out if his feelings had changed now that they weren't undercover, or if, like her, he wanted… well, more.

"Thanks for staying with me."

"You're family," Luna said. "Of course we're going to be here."

Lee smiled at them both. One thing that was different about being betrayed by someone she trusted was *this family* and having the self-confidence to know that she hadn't messed anything up. Boyd was playing a different game and he'd used her, but he'd paid for it.

"You guys can go home now if you want," Lee said after a few more minutes had passed.

"Or maybe just go to the hall and send Aaron in?" Luna asked with a smirk. "Come on, Van, let's go."

Van kissed her forehead and Luna gave her a gentle hug before they both left. Lee was nervous as she waited for Aaron to come in, and it seemed he was too. He entered the room and then leaned against the wall, just watching her.

He'd had time to change, wearing one of his fancy vests with pants that were tailored to fit him perfectly. His hair was perfectly styled, the sleeves of his dress shirt rolled up to reveal his muscled forearms.

She lifted her hand out to him and he rushed to her side. Their eyes met, and she sensed he was feeling the same wild cocktail of emotions she was.

"I love you," he said. "That's probably not what you expected to hear from me. But I do."

"I love you too," she whispered. "I don't know how to make this work, or if it even will work out, but I want to try."

He leaned over her, careful not to nudge her side, resting his forehead against hers. "I'm so horrible at relationships, and a part of me knows I shouldn't risk it, but I can't *not* risk it. I am not letting you go."

Her heart beat faster, and she felt warm and fuzzy inside in a way that she'd never experienced before. She could think of no better man to be with than Aaron. He had weathered so much in his life and kept moving through it and getting stronger.

She had no doubts he'd do the same with his relationship with her.

"I'm not great at relationships either. We'll figure it out as we go along and make one that works for us."

Us.

She loved the sound of that almost as much as she loved him. He climbed up onto the bed with her, pulling her gently into his arms. The way he held her made her feel safe, cherished even. Two things she hadn't felt in a long time, maybe ever, until she'd stumbled into his undercover op and started fake dating him.

There was nothing fake about the way he kissed her or the emotions in his eyes as he held her until she drifted off to sleep, secure that she'd finally found a home of her own with this man she loved so much.

* * * * *

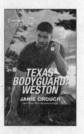